THE AFTERNOON SUN

THE AFTERNOON SUN

David Pryce-Jones

WEIDENFELD & NICOLSON
NEW YORK

Published by Weidenfeld & Nicolson, New York
A Division of Wheatland Corporation
10 East 53rd Street
New York, NY 10022

Originally published in Great Britain in 1986
by George Weidenfeld & Nicolson Limited

LIBRARY OF CONGRESS CATALOGING-IN-PUBLICATION DATA
Pryce-Jones, David, 1936-
The afternoon sun.
I. Title.
PR6066.R88A64   1986   823'.914   86-9068
ISBN 1-55584-006-X

Manufactured in the United States of America
First American Edition 1986
10 9 8 7 6 5 4 3 2 1

THE AFTERNOON SUN

· Prologue ·

Gustav Ellingen was a legend in his day. How was it done? The question was put to him even by people born to privileges and therefore without real interest in those who had made their own way. His answers were not always the same, and that too was legendary.

'Once an orphan always an orphan,' he might say. 'To have nothing to lose is the beginning of true opportunity.'

'But you are a famous industrialist, a landowner, one of the richest men in the country. In the streets they point at you driving past and say, there goes Gustav Ellingen.'

'Measures must be taken at all times to avoid the stupidity of others.'

At least he was fulfilled, and if he was not fulfilled, at least he was successful. In the example, there was hope. Those listening to Gustav Ellingen, in the course of doing business with him or at one of his dinners, perceived how his own story touched in him a wonder for the gift of life.

Essential to the phenomenon was his physical appearance. He was not much more than five foot. No tailor could hide the unbalanced shape. More than greed, the appetite was an expression of vitality. As others might exercise, so he ate. Veal, for half an hour, he once replied to a head-waiter who had asked what he wanted to order. When he sat in a chair, his legs and knees were pressed apart by the weight of flesh. Putting on or taking off his shoes involved a dressing-room ritual, with Burschen Franz, always so nicknamed, or Boy Franz, his valet, kneeling on the floor.

Early in life he had lost his hair. Only grizzled stubble remained, in a line like a water-mark. Sensitive on this single aspect of his appearance, he had the habit of running a hand over his scalp in disbelief at its smoothness. The head was too massive to be ugly. A wide mouth, with lips set into expressions between humour, irony, sensuality, changing at a twitch. Pink skin, unlined, as in someone much younger. And then the eyes, which in colour were neither quite blue nor quite green, pale as stone, focusing apparently on faraway things unseen by others. Those astonishing eyes watered easily as he cried and laughed about himself.

Prince Solkovsky, his crony, liked to bellow in front of guests or acquaintances, 'Tell them how old you are.'

Casting back over what had happened, Gustav Ellingen concluded that he had been born either in 1839 or 1840. He had no known birth-date to celebrate.

'You have to be very lucky,' he might say, 'or very old, before you bring yourself to believe in destiny.'

Chance at every turn, then, as on the day when Gustav had been in the Concordia office and a caller was announced, Prince Felix Solkovsky, according to the engraved card.

Without preliminaries, Solkovsky had given away his thoughts – 'Show me round this factory.'

'Do we owe the honour of this visit to gambling losses, or what?'

'The iron and steel business is too important politically and strategically to be left in the hands of Jews, and you know that.'

A man of imposing physique, Solkovsky towered over Gustav. His beard was in the style of the Prince of Wales, the future Edward VII. Smoking cigars, both men had walked round the plant, the furnaces, rolling-mills, stock-yard, the railway siding. Several hundred men were already employed at Concordia, and it was Gustav's boast that he knew every one of them by name.

'I'm thirty-four,' Solkovsky said. 'By the time I'm fifty I shall be prime minister.'

In his statesman's manner, the voice theatrically low, he predicted the rise and fall of thrones and governments – as a result of which Concordia would also rise or fall. The national mission was to expand into the Balkans, by arrangement. It was 1886 when Solkovsky organised the visit to St Petersburg. A private coach was hitched to the train. Relations of Solkovsky's had them to stay in a palace with a staircase of onyx. The audience with the Czar was at Pavlovsk. As the allotted thirty minutes stretched over more than an hour, the Czar did not once mention steel requirements, confining himself to trivialities, notably the differences between Austrian and Russian infantry uniforms. A silver cigarette box was presented to Gustav. Until the eve of the war, Russian experts came regularly to the factory with specifications and orders.

On the way home, Gustav stared out of the train windows across desolate plains, lugubrious forests. This landscape so affronted the spirit within him that he recalled it with horror to the end of his life. At Prague, the private coach was routed along the line to Pressburg, to within a few miles of Rentzenburg, where Solkovsky lived. In the eighteenth century, parts of a medieval castle had been torn down, and a baroque house constructed within the fortifications. There was a private chapel. The old *Rittersaal* had survived and one entire wall of it was painted with a family tree on which, at the appropriate places alongside red lettering in gothic capitals, hung portraits in gilt oval frames.

'A hundred and twenty-eight quarterings,' Solkovsky said. 'Enough for us both.'

Princess Irina, his wife, stayed at Rentzenburg all round the year. After a mass in the chapel, every morning she rode sidesaddle on her white mare. Had society allowed it, she would have liked to be a gardener, a botanist, university-educated. Failing that, she longed only to be a mother. Fifteen more years were to pass before the Solkovsky son, Paul, was born, too late to redeem disappointment. The Princess Irina rose, named after her, is a pale yellow, the broad-petalled variety.

'How can you trust someone like Felix ?' she asked Gustav. 'With him it's a failing, he so badly wants to be a great man.'

Since the Phoenicians invented paper, Solkovsky explained to Gustav during that first stay at Rentzenburg, there had been a recognisable way of rewarding services, and he expected Concordia shares.

My *Renommiergoy*. My *Hausjude*.

Prince Solkovsky was almost fifty, and had settled for money rather than politics, when he accompanied Gustav to another imperial audience, this time in the Hofburg, on 2 June 1904, according to the record of appointments, at half past eleven.

Kaiser Franz Josef straightened himself up as he asked – 'How will your horse run in the Derby?'

'Better next year, *Majestät*, when he'll be at the top of his form.'

Like everybody else, the old emperor hoped to fasten on some memorable formula, for he added – 'What is your secret?'

'Avoiding the stupidities of others.'

A sigh followed, and the emperor said – 'To reward those who deserve it, my dear friend, is the most enjoyable part of my duties.'

A red morocco box was presented, with in it a patent of nobility for Baron Gustav.

More than anyone, Solkovsky liked to tell stories about Gustav, and dramatise their friendship. In doing so, he made sure to say 'The best of the joke is that our little Gustav probably isn't Jewish at all.'

·*Part One*·

·One·

Gustav had been given the first name of the German carter who had picked him up in a crib abandoned on the side of a road. This had happened outside the small town of Ellingen, hence the surname. On the child's coat a note had been pinned that here was a Jewish baby, to be delivered to the Waisenhaus in Nuremberg.

'I try to remember how the beginning was' – this is the version handed down from Gustav – 'and I see yellow bricks, a chimney-stack, a dormitory wall, I cannot be sure which. The whole world outside looked as solid and blank as that wall, there had to be a way through. Every month a razor was put to the head of each and every one of us, down to the smallest. You've noticed how I rub the top of my head? The razor had a rasp that sent cold shivers down the spine. Lice were our greatest shame, we picked them off each other, they are hard to squash between the finger-nails. Each spring, and again in the autumn, new clothes were distributed because some bene-factor had left an endowment for the purpose. We stood in line. The boots were deliberately too large so that we could grow into them ... you could always spot one of us on account of our shuffling in those boots. Still we had to pray for the benefactor of blessed memory. And the matron in-sisted that this was a great mercy, that in the world plenty of children were barefoot. The blankets that we folded on our beds were like animal hides, they were so stiff. We slept on boards, with straw mattresses. They taught us trades, and to be good Jews. Every day we said prayers. *Shma Israel Adonai Eloheynu Adonai Echad* ... Our teacher threw himself into it, a poor wretch in a gabardine, only now I realise that his was the feverish face of hunger, tuberculosis maybe ... *Jude muss man sein aber nicht zum Abattoir*, one must be a Jew but not go to the slaughter-house for it. I must have been ten or eleven when I ran away, with my friend Moritz, who had known his mother and father and couldn't believe they had died or forsaken him. He was convinced he'd been kidnapped. I was never unhappy like that. We hoarded up biscuits and slipped out. He made off for what he imagined his home. Not to be caught together, I chose the opposite direction. With my back to the afternoon sun.'

Had it not been for Moritz and his imagination, then, Gustav Ellingen might have played his part in Bismarck's Germany, or further to the west, in the France of Louis Napoleon and the Third Republic. Sometimes Gustav was in the mood to glory in his exploits on the run, how he had lifted rabbits by the ears from their hutches, or guinea-fowl, eggs from farmyards, dug up potatoes, flushing at the footsteps of someone who might discover him – how he had accompanied a pedlar and travelled in Bohemia and Moravia to earn his keep, how he had been apprenticed to a carpenter in a village called Hradek and had a scar on the elbow to prove it, how he had worked a loom in the Iglau mills.

'The road came to a bridge across a river, I waited to be sure I was alone. On the far side stood a gallows and on that gallows a man hung in the wind. How did I know that this had been a Hungarian rebel? It's a fact, it proved I had reached Habsburg lands. The boots had been stolen, the bones of the feet dangled. A Hungarian. There's an instinct about these things. Once I was picking fruit in an orchard and had not realised that a woman was watching. A big woman, quite young, with a scarf tied over her hair. Jew, she was screaming at me as she moved to catch me, but I broke away through a hole in the hedge. How had she jumped to the conclusion that I was a Jew? Instinct again.'

To describe to the rich and respectable how necessity had driven him to theft remained a life-long pleasure – Only those who have stolen to keep alive have the right to speak about honesty.

This maxim acquired a more mature expression – Never speak of a million until you have made one.

When at length he entered Vienna, the city was still walled, soldiers patrolled its ramparts, artillery and cavalry manoeuvres were held below the glacis in open countryside. Sixty years on, nostalgia for the lost capital possessed him: *that* was the place, *those* were the times.

Out of a window a woman had beckoned.

'Hannah had been married to Max Schlesinger long enough to be afraid she'd never have children. They wanted an errand-boy but really it was a son they were after. The women I've known always wanted a dozen children when the fact was they could hardly have one. Hannah smiled at me out of a ground-floor window on the Rabanplatz, life was never the same afterwards. I had a room in that house. Brothers and sisters on both sides used to stay for months at a time. I came to know what a family might be.'

A portrait of Max Schlesinger survives in the museum in Vienna which is devoted to the history of the city. In the museum catalogue, Schlesinger is described as the descendant of Jewish merchants from Germany, founder of a bank which after his death was absorbed into the Wiener Wechselbank. His dates are given as 1814 to 1879. The picture, painted in 1869 by one of the von Alts, formalises the sitter in an interior which suggests luxury strictly within the bounds of conventionality. The table beside him has a tasselled covering as dark and intricate as the Persian carpet underfoot. In spite of his age at the time of sitting for the portrait, Schlesinger's hair was grey only at the temples, brushed forward in curls in the fashion of his youth. Cautious geniality is caught in his attitude.

Hannah endured long years of widowhood. Gustav used to send a carriage for her, she dined with him on Sundays. Their affair, as the gossips put it, looked set to outlast the empire.

·*Two*·

In the 1850s a remarkable priest began teaching at the Schotten Gymnasium. Pater Gschwandt was a latter-day romantic, the open-air kind, in communion with Nature. Certain poems by Goethe and Byron influenced him to write rhapsodies in verse about the Wienerwald and the Danube, the pleasures of walking in picturesque mountains and of harvesting the hay. From these verses to a cloudy pan-German nationalism was a short step. A reputation grew. A circle developed around Pater Gschwandt with the purpose of holding up the Teutons of a mythical past as moral exemplars in the present. These exalted proselytisers have been the subject of intensive research because one of them was Georg von Schönerer, leading anti-semite of the day, destined to be influential in the formation of the character of Hitler.

For this reason Pater Gschwandt's correspondence was collected and published in Leipzig in 1927, long after his death and too late for Gustav to read it.

On August 12 1854 the priest was writing to Baroness Antonina Beck, a patron.

You know the little Jew of whom I have had such high hopes this past year. A most intelligent boy, he has all the aptitudes of his tribe, and a frank and fearless manner with it. Unwearyingly I argue his case with his mentor Schlesinger. How much preferable were the sons of Abraham when they worshipped the golden calf openly in the desert! Healthier by far to observe these collective outbursts. Amongst us they bear themselves as though they had never danced or sang, but only been chastised for the worship of false gods. Can they really be without interest in our culture and manners? Schlesinger gives that impression, he keeps a tight hold of the foundling, he thinks his protégé has genius. Apparently he is teaching himself French and English in leaps and bounds. So I am not to recover him again.

27 September 1854, to Baroness Beck.

With your incomparable generosity and humanity, you may achieve the miracle for which I am hoping on the part of my little Jew. In Stredlitz he will be imbued with the God-given calm of the righteous, and this cannot fail to impress him. Last Wednesday he called here in the Gymnasium, we spoke right through the afternoon. No allowances can be made for a pupil who is not of the faith, therefore his spiritual progress is urgent. The Jew astonished me with a discourse about Jacobinism on the one hand and Russian autocracy on the other. The twin evils of the age are apparent to this goblin of a fellow, for whom I could form a strong attachment, if only his heart were the size of his head. But unregenerate! The beauty of Stredlitz will touch him at several levels, I trust. Should the chamber orchestra play, then include Papa Haydn, for all other music, he comically asserts, is a trick against his taste.

2 September 1856, to Frau T. Desfours zu Athienville, sister of Baroness Beck.

With a number of my pupils, including your devoted nephew, we have completed a most charming excursion. Neither the Italians nor French, nor even the vaunted Swiss, have scenery to boast of superior to our beloved Kratzenspitz, the dear Mönchsberg with its ravines and crags, the entire valley in the glimmering depths which amongst ourselves we know as the *Mephistophelestal.* The Dietrichstein boy, star of my class, made a last valiant effort with the little Jew. We were seated in an Alpine meadow, the buttercups and daisies as bright as the brightest jewels. My Jew defended himself in a manly spirit, I must admit, but his heart was hardened. In anger, his eyes are truly most exceptional, as steady and unmoving as a glacier. I felt myself bruised, then crushed, by the glare that bore down on me. He has taken umbrage. We shall not see him again. To the counting-house, my little Gustav, to the copy-book and ledger, to usury among the stiff-necked Hebrews. Disappointment spreads to those we cherish at Stredlitz, and for my part I will not hide my feelings. *O formose puer, nimium ne crede colori.*

·*Three*·

In his twenties Gustav became the partner of Schlesinger. Those happened to be years of consolidation, the so-called *Gründerzeit*. If the city was to expand, brickworks had to be commissioned. If beet was to be grown in industrial quantities, railways had to be laid to transport the crop. Schlesinger had contacts with Alois Miesbach, the brick king, and with Alexander Schoeller, the sugar manufacturer. Previously a specialist in discounting bills he moved into financing joint-stock companies, dealing with the new capitalists, Eskeles, Sima, Wodianer, the Haber brothers, Count Kinsky; and with the Crédit Mobilier, the Anglo-Austrian Bank, the Imperial Gas Company. Outgrowing the Rabanplatz premises, the bank transferred into a building recently completed on the Kolowratring.

Gustav might have remained one among thousands of bankers and dealers on the money-market, had it not been for the stock-exchange collapse of 1873. Capitalist speculation created that crisis. In one venture after another, paper credit had been issued without real assets to back it. As the artificial boom fell apart, quotations dropped within a matter of days by hundreds of millions of florins. Over a hundred bankruptcies were declared. On settlement day of that account, shares could hardly be disposed of. What had begun as doubt ended in despair and a record number of suicides.

No recovery was likely even in the medium term, according to Schlesinger, capitalism itself was flawed, the socialists and revolutionaries had had their theories tested and proved correct.

Gustav disagreed – 'Select sound stocks and buy at rock-bottom prices.'

'When the roof falls, the man who gets out through the door lives another day,' Max Schlesinger said. In that crucial week, he lost the savings of a life-time. Without Hannah as go-between, the breach might have been final. A humiliated Schlesinger lived to realise how mistaken his judgement had been, but not long enough to bring himself to make up the quarrel.

'Sell to the sound of violins, buy to the sound of cannon.'

Gustav's original remark, or some variation of it, remains today in every stock-broker's vocabulary. He raised whatever money he could, some proportion of it certainly paid by Schlesinger to buy out the partnership. For sums which had no relation to real values, he bought into productive companies which were certain to continue trading profitably once speculative positions had been sorted out. As that fateful month of May 1873 dragged out in extended crisis, he was virtually alone to enter the Stock Exchange as a buyer.

It was a nine-day wonder.

The *Neue Wiener Tagblatt*, launched only six years earlier at the height of the expansion, carried this sketch on June 4 1873, all in the style upon which its reputation was built.

We have witnessed bankruptcies, we have fled from suicides. We have observed men accustomed to gargantuan repasts who will feast no more, who are indeed at this moment pawning their frock-coats for garments more suitable to the soup-kitchens in which they will have to fast in future. Carriages roll away from the Bourse bearing in them those who believed that natural laws had been suspended for their benefit, and that what went up never came down again. How piquant to uncover such superstition among those vaunted for their sophistication.

One carriage remains, however, from dawn to dusk. Gustav Ellingen is at his post. For many a wretch, he is the last hope. Indeed a spectacle! For who exactly is this saviour? An orphan from the Kingdom of Bavaria, who arrived among us, so we are reliably informed, nameless and shameless and, more to the point, penniless. Hofrat Max Schlesinger allowed himself to be beguiled by the undoubted dynamism of this unusual immigrant, and engaged him as a penny-a-line clerk, little realising that a phenomenon, not to say a household favourite, was in the making. Few young men so brilliant have lately done our capital such honour, and even fewer have been interested in philanthropy. Already Herr Ellingen looks unnaturally aged, whether through the pressures of optimism or the excessive application of his talents. The money he hands out, as and when enthusiasm seizes him, is understood not to be Hofrat Schlesinger's – the head of that honourable and conservative house, in which Herr Ellingen no longer holds a partnership, is, we learn, exclusively studying the telegraphic bulletins of the Paris Bourse and Threadneedle Street, while consoling himself that in the past he has thoughtfully gratified his wife's taste for diamonds, a commodity which may vanish into paste in these difficult and dangerous times, but hardly into thin air.

By the end of the year, confidence had returned. As the market stabilised, Gustav rationalised his holdings. Over a period of five or six years, he concentrated on rail-roads. Having bought the concession, he constructed and for a while operated the Wodnan-Prachatitz line. Also the Strakonitz-Winterberg line, the Warsaw by-pass, the Lemberg-Czernovitz-Jassy line. In different rail-road undertakings, he participated with the Rothschilds through their Compagnie du Nord. In 1882 he was guest of honour at the opening of the Hernalser-Währinger line, of which he also became chairman. These developments, and others of the kind, are recorded in the *Geschichte der Eisenbahnen Oesterreiches*, an official history in five volumes of railways in the Habsburg empire. Tamed, the *Neue Wiener Tagblatt* appears to have confined itself to mentioning Gustav in the society columns. On June 7 1878, it is recorded that he contributed fifty thousand florins to the construction of the Ottakring hospital. The following year, he is reported to be travelling through Dalmatia, with the intention of examining railway prospects in Montenegro and Hercegovina.

Having no home, he reserved a suite in the Imperial Hotel. There he brooded, there he consolidated. The Locomotiv-Fabrik-Aktien Gesellschaft had been acquired during the crash for a fraction of its value. The company was contracted to supply rolling-stock to the railways, thereby breaking an English monopoly. Pioneering days were coming to a close in the rail-roads. Gustav decided to remove the factory from

Gross-Jedlersdorf to a new and more convenient site north-east of Vienna. This great venture, the Gustav-Ellingen-Metallwerke, was more generally known as Concordia. At the centre of the new plant, set in a court-yard, a three-storey building was put up in which Gustav at last had offices, and living quarters in which he could spend the night.

Of Eduard von Arnheim, Concordia's first Director-General, the old Brockdorff Lexicon says that he was born in Klausenburg, or Kluj, into a family granted its rank for service to the Habsburgs. Engineering studies in England, at Leeds; joined Gelsenkirchner Bergwerks on whose behalf he had surveyed Silesian coal and Swedish iron ore deposits; introduced into Austria the modern technology of steel-making, including the first Siemens-Martin oven to be built outside Germany. Married in 1878 and had a son, also called Eduard. In a notorious speech at a conference of industrialists in Basel in 1891 he predicted that Concordia in the following century would rival the Ruhr concerns.

·*Four*·

'You risk becoming an eccentric,' Solkovsky warned Gustav. 'Hiding yourself away in a hotel room is no social base. It is your weak point. People can't help being curious about you.'

This was said in the autumn after the journey to St Petersburg, and Solkovsky was in possession of his Concordia shares. The receptions to which Solkovsky dragged him were identical, Gustav complained, the guests were as interchangeable as the brocade curtains across the windows or the chandeliers suspended from the ceilings.

Across such a room Gustav saw a woman. He knew neither her name nor whether she was single or already married. None of his investments had been as impulsive as what he said to her by way of introduction.

'Ever since I ran away from the Nuremberg orphanage, I have made friends by chance. Whenever the time was right. Whenever I needed to. The time is right now to meet you.'

The strength of his emotions pushed tears into the corners of his eyes, and he had to dab at them with his handkerchief.

Else Dreinach was taller than Gustav. That she could stand up to him, in every sense, may explain why he fell in love. Everything about her face was on a masculine rather than feminine scale : the full chin, fleshy lips, commanding brown eyes with heavy eyebrows. Her hair, properly black, and long though worn braided, drew attention away from a complexion which was pallid, as though from secret suffering which she was too proud to share, even with Gustav.

Calling upon her father, Gustav found himself in one of the old-fashioned houses of a generation earlier, when new wealth had first to be converted into respectability and status. In his own rooms, Professor Theodor Dreinach had taken to a wheel-chair, he did not stand up for his future son-in-law. A rug covered his knees. His hands trembled slightly.

'Since I became a widower, Else has been caring for me, we lead a very quiet life. I have my work. You realise that she has been engaged once before, her fiancé proved consumptive.'

'So she has informed me.'

'She likes to read, and is fond of music.'

'Unfortunately I have no such tastes, I have never had time for them. If you are saying that I am marrying above myself, you are right.'

'Should all go well, and I am granted even my poor health for another ten years, then I shall have completed my history of the folk migrations of the Dark Ages. Gepids, Alans, Visigoths, Pechenegs, these names mean more to me than that of Prince Solkovsky, your colleague, or of his friend Count Badeni, the prime minister.'

When Else entered the drawing-room, she carried copies of learned journals in which articles of her father's had been published. Deliberately, Gustav left them behind on the table. It would have been hypocrisy for him to pretend to have been willing or able to learn from such writings.

As a present to mark their engagement, Else gave him a miniature of herself, painted on wood, and set in a frame carved to represent a wreath of flowers. For this portrait she had chosen to wear a dress of green silk, with black trimmings, its bodice accentuating rather than flattering her waist and bosom. On the back of this miniature Gustav pasted a tiny note – the script beautifully legibile – the sole such personal touch of hers to have survived: 'My beloved, when I am not with you in person, then my spirit will be here to stand guard over you, to keep you from all evil, so that the two of us are united, come what may.'

Conventions are what they are, and the advantages of marrying Gustav will not have passed unnoticed, but those are the words of a woman not content with a marriage of convenience, a woman of feeling and even passion.

The ceremony was held in the Seitenstettengasse synagogue. In the custom of the period, wedding presents and their

donors were listed in the society columns of newspapers –
glass from Lobmayr's, silver and silver-gilt from Klingenho-
fer's, jewellery from Korff's or Moritz Oesterreicher's. From
the widowed Hannah Schlesinger, gold-rimmed Bohemian
glass. From Prince and Princess Solkovsky, a pair of silver
tureens. From Eduard von Arnheim, the skin of a tiger shot in
the Dutch East Indies. The Archduke Karl Ludwig, the capitalist Count Kinsky, Count Badeni and another prime minister Count Taaffe, were among those drawn on to those
newspaper lists by the power of Concordia.

In wedding photographs Gustav is standing well to the
fore, evidently in order to diminish Else's height. For the first
night, they travelled no further than his suite in the Imperial
Hotel. A double-window opened on to a balcony, and they
stepped out.

'Which of the houses in sight would you like?' Gustav
asked.

On the honeymoon proper, Gustav arranged with a
laundry in London that in future his shirts would be posted
once a week from Vienna, and returned starched like an
English gentleman's. A chemist accepted a standing order for
Grimshaw's talcum-powder, with its scent of violets. Paris,
by contrast, bored him : the place was best admired from a
distance, he said. For Else's sake, in Berlin he attended the
opera twice, but never again in his life.

In those first improvised weeks of marriage Gustav re-
enacted in luxury what once he had experienced on the open
road in hardship and hunger.

'Money prevents fear, that's its point. Those with the greatest fears need the greatest wealth.'

'In our family things turn out unlucky. You have yet to discover what bad luck is, the orphanage ought to warn you
about the poor-house. What if Concordia fails one day? You
won't be able to control it. You have competitors, enemies,
maybe even Solkovsky who is so pleased to call himself your
friend.'

'Let us enjoy ourselves then, if only for fear of the worst.'

His extravagance dated from his marriage. The increasing

appetite at meals was only an aspect of the acquisitive urge.

One night in the Imperial Hotel Else woke him up, shivering, whispering 'I'm in pain, I don't believe I can bear it.' Lighting the gas lamp, he saw how a stain was spreading wide over the sheets. This was blood which ought to have become their flesh, a child, his descendant, an heir.

'Look on her as an invalid,' the doctor said. 'Your wife has a poor constitution. The gynaecologist, I am confident, will tell you both not to attempt a family.'

The blankness in Gustav's eyes was formidable, not registering either the words he was hearing or the consequences to be foreseen.

Primarius Fleischmann, already gaining an international reputation as one of the pioneers of obstetric surgery, did not concur. More than a consultant, he became a friend, champion of the gestation and safe delivery of an Ellingen heir. Like Gustav, he considered will-power to be some sort of absolute. 'She will be all right,' he told Gustav, 'because no other alternative can be considered.'

It was recommended that they live outside the city, in healthier air. In his impatience, Gustav ordered a young man by the name of Leo Margulies, from the Concordia accounts department, to find whatever might be suitable. Sometimes they drove together to inspect possibilities. Beyond Hietzing, then still a village not yet incorporated into Vienna, lay Pernsdorf, where twenty-four hectares of land were available. Fine old trees, mostly beech and silver birch, and a lake which had half-seeped away under wild water-lilies and reeds. If indeed this was a ruined estate, no trace of a house remained. From the undergrowth a fox emerged, on a path within a few feet of Gustav and Margulies.

'Here we could build exactly what we want.'

'I'd always imagined myself in a room looking on to a lake,' Else said.

'That's that, then,' Gustav said.

Siccardsburg and van der Null were architects who had become controversial for their conception of the Burgtheater. The one had died of a heart attack, the other had committed suicide in the face of professional criticism. At an auction to dispose of the contents of their studio, Gustav purchased drawings of a fantastic villa dreamed up for themselves rather than as a practical proposition for a client. 'It's as if the pair of them had known me for years,' Gustav said, 'and could see right into me. This is my house.' A *baumeister* was appointed. Immediately clay was laid to stabilise the bottom of the lake. Within a new surrounding wall, the park was landscaped, the thickets cleared, a drive designed and asphalted, a lodge prepared. Under the terms of a strict contract, everything had to be ready within a calendar year.

What was known as 'the Ellingen Schloss' rose. Only a romantic could have realised something of the kind, with its elaboration of design, lack of symmetry, variety of material and shapes and angles. Self-confidence on this scale was beyond the reach of criticism. The ground floor was in a brown stone quarried in rectangular blocks. Above, the facades were adorned with stucco and inset timbering. The steep pitch of the roof, in slate almost mauve in colour, was broken by belfries, towers, pepper-pots.

An enormous central hall, in effect a domestic version of a stage, dominated the interior. Around it were the *salons*, the dining-room and smaller reception rooms. In one of these was a billiard table, not that Gustav or his friends played – 'I had to have it to go with Eduard's tiger skin,' Gustav used to say. Out of the hall, a staircase wide enough for a dozen people abreast swept up to a gallery. The entire central feature was lit from above by a dome too flat to be visible from the exterior, the glass tinted a yellowy brown, creating mysteries and shadows. Along one side of the gallery, Else's rooms overlooked the park and lake, as intended, with a matching set of rooms for Gustav opposite. Higher, among the patch-work of eaves and turrets were nurseries for children, quarters for servants, guest-rooms.

Else was not to be disturbed, Gustav said, she was resting in order to regain her strength. For much of 1889, she lived in a rented house at Ischl, where he joined her to escape the heat of summer. Pernsdorf was his house ; from first to last, he gave the orders : panelling and parquet floorings, six identical Tolentino marble chimney-places especially commissioned for the large rooms downstairs, satin curtains with swags and pelmets, four-posters, chandeliers, lacquer screens in the Japanese taste, potted plants. Like a theatrical backdrop, in the stairwell hung a larger-than-life picture by Lecomte-du-Nouy of an Arab prince on a piebald horse, attended by bodyguards, lances in hand, at the outset of a noble procession through the desert. Exhibited in Paris, the picture had been much commented on, and Gustav bid for it by telegram. 'Your Semitic kinsman,' Solkovsky remarked, initiating an association of thought common to virtually everyone who climbed the four steps at the entrance up to the front door.

Gustav offered his arm to Else, to lead her up those four steps. Waiting to be introduced were the house-keeper and butler, Burschen Franz the valet, footmen, maids, the head-gardener. Side by side, at a table capable of seating twenty-four, Else and Gustav dined alone.

She asked, 'How am I going to live up to this?'

The answer was 'By our children, and our children's children.'

'If I didn't know you, I would guess that you must have ruined yourself. What can people be saying about us?'

Professor Dreinach, their first guest, pointed out that there was no library. A room downstairs would be converted, shelving installed. Gustav asked him to order whatever books were required.

'That will be my contribution to your well-being,' the professor said. Well before the book-cases were ready, parcels from Nebenzahl, the specialist dealer, began to arrive.

Sometimes Gustav returned to sleep in his bachelor room in the Concordia offices. The factory was at its peak, employing over a thousand men, exporting to new markets in the Ottoman empire, to America, even to Australia. On occasions, Gustav and Eduard von Arnheim were away for weeks at a stretch, in Germany, Italy, England.

Afterwards he accused himself of lack of foresight – why had he assumed that because Else was in Pernsdorf she could

25

safely expect a child? How had he come to disregard the miscarriage? In her pregnancy she had done nothing more strenuous than stroll round the lake or give instructions for planting vegetables in the kitchen garden, as yet unfinished, or watch the completion of the stable block.

Only in the final month was there apprehension. Something was amiss. Was it irresponsible of the gynaecologist not to have transferred Else to the Rudolphinum clinic? At the onset of labour, she could be heard crying, with panic in the voice. Chloroform for a difficult birth. Gustav pushed into the room, for a sight of his daughter, a creature with thick black hair across her forehead like her mother's. He held Else's hand, and believed that she still recognised him. Next time he saw her, they were changing her, the legs were exposed, such white inanimate flesh – the flanks of a pole-axed animal.

'Do you choose between mother and child?'

Primarius Fleischmann confronted Gustav with the words, 'Medicine offers no such choice.'

Gustav no longer trusted the doctors, he was unable to concentrate on clinical details. On the last day of March 1891 Else died, without recovering for any exchange of words, without once holding the new-born Henriette in her arms.

As Else lay on her death-bed, Gustav gave orders that the lights throughout the house should be lit, and remain burning while he was there, whenever he was there. Not a single room was to stay in the dark. Until the end of his life, shutters were to be left open, in winter especially, so that as he turned in past the lodge and up the drive, he could see lights shining everywhere in the silhouette of his home, in simulation of welcome.

· Five ·

Grief takes a man as it may. Gustav concentrated on his fortune. Two of the ground-floor rooms at Pernsdorf were converted into private offices for his assistants, Brühl and Leviseur, and Margulies, promoted to confidential advisor, with Fräulein Lindner as secretary. Avoidance of stupidity in orders was also Margulies's philosophy. 'We must put money abroad,' he said, 'and stick to primary production, invest in minerals, Congo copper, gold, and diamond fields.' The question to be decided, according to Solkovsky, was which would happen first, war with Russia or a revolution. The streets would run with blood, 1848 would seem a trifle.

Grund fliegt nimmer weg – land never flies away. An estate had to be found, as security. The right property. The occasion to buy arose when Gustav was approached by a Hungarian. Sandor von Pechy himself lived in western Hungary, at Felsöjattö, sixty miles south of Gyor. Not far away was Sagodvar, a village, four thousand hectares, a stud. The bankrupt owner made it a condition of sale that the stud and the racehorses be maintained.

'In return for a commission, I will guarantee that you are elected to the Jockey Club.'

Whether or not Sandor von Pechy was in earnest when he said this, the facts were that Gustav bought Sagodvar without ever having set foot in the place, that he did not pay a commission, and was elected to the Jockey Club within eighteen months. Hardly had the deed been signed, moreover, than Bludan, a two-year-old, won the Crown-Prince-Rudolph Stakes at Budapest. Nothing to do with Concordia had previously placed Gustav's name so prominently before the public at large. As racing colours, he had selected a Prussian

27

blue with a gold band, and gold cap. At the races he favoured a bowler hat, in the English custom. The *Illustrierte* and sporting papers and periodicals played up the quirks of this newest of owners. Caricatures of him were published, the stomach like a globe, a cigar puffing vertically like the stack of a railway engine, binoculars weighing him down. His racing showed a profit, however.

La Société de Vienne was a collection of sketches and essays well received in its day, and often reprinted, with a companion volume entitled *La Société de Berlin*. In its 1895 edition appears a record of Gustav Ellingen, under a chapter with the heading 'Finanzjuden'. The author of this informative book presented himself as a Russian, Comte Vassili, a pseudonym behind which, so he implied, was hidden the illegitimate son of the Czar or at least a Grand Duke. *Nouveau riche* was not a distinction to distress this unusual commentator, who welcomed careerists.

Few among them (*i.e.* successfully assimilated Jews) have displayed the flair of Gustav Ellingen, who may claim to be among the most Chosen of these People. His origins are of the humblest. I have heard it said that for many years he has resisted Austro-Hungarian citizenship on the grounds that no passport he might ever possess would supercede the identity of Wandering Jew. The reproach that his fortune is grounded in the misfortune of others hardly bears examination. His cool-headed capacities and foresight were exercised in the dark year of 1873, when the threat to public financing heralded scarcely less than that lapse into anarchy which even its friends and supporters often predict with alarm for the empire. Concessions and companies bought at the then depressed prices have been seen to multiply a hundred and a thousand-fold. No *Finanzjude* in the sense of enriching himself by shuffling paper, Ellingen has become one of the new and prominent industrialists whom the powers of Europe ignore at their peril.

His peers, *Messieurs les barons* Wertheimstein, Todesco, Koenigswarter, Oppenheim, tend to shun him. Nobody so rich, they pretend, has the right to be so unprepossessing physically, or to build for himself such a monstrosity of taste as the Pernsdorfer Schloss. This house, it is true, the last word in Jewish vulgarity, has been much mocked, not least by those more than willing to receive hospitality there. This is thoroughly in keeping with the Viennese spirit, a quality which in other civilised countries is described as malice. Remarks concerning his personal appearance are a particular source of vexation, and references to his baldness unsettle him altogether. Vanity on this score compels him to have his hair cut frequently, or more exactly, to go through the motions of doing so, for his pate might well be more interesting in its smoothness to a naturalist than to a barber. Amusingly, any servant who says that Ellingen has been that day to the barber, and is in the right, may claim a crown as a reward, conversely having it deducted from his wages if the guess is mistaken.

In matters social and political, Ellingen is greatly under the thumb of Prince Felix Solkovsky. This nobleman has more than his fair share of rascality, Polish rascality to boot. Whether such a man is the fit model for a Jewish entrepreneur to imitate only time will tell, but the integration of Jews with Austro-Hungary – of this example most notably – owes much to the sponsorship of men such as Solkovsky. Solkovsky it was who introduced Ellingen to St Petersburg in 1886. I have it from Count Ignatieff himself that on that occasion the Czar expressed surprise that such a pair should travel in amity, to each other's commercial advantage.

Jews in Russia, Comte Vassili went on, too often had themselves to blame for the contemptuous way they were treated. Friendship with a Jew, he considered, was most unlikely, though he took pains to distance himself from anti-semitism. Unexpectedly he commented that hatred for Jews was far more immediate in the Habsburg empire than in Russia, and in the long run more disturbing. Nothing of the kind had been perceptible twenty years earlier when he had begun his experiences of Vienna and Jews had been more segregated. This gossip-minded Russian aristocrat (if such he was in fact) concluded that the energy and creativity of Jews like Gustav Ellingen did not serve primarily as an example of model citizenship, but rather emphasised the failure of other people to move with the times.

·Six·

On fine days, when the pram was wheeled out into the park and down to the lake, Gustav, if he passed, might pause to raise the muslin net for a glimpse of the black-haired child underneath. When it was the season for Sagodvar, he left Henriette behind at Pernsdorf, with the nanny, Miss Magoffin, Guffy, from Dumfries. Without explanation, he might be away travelling elsewhere for weeks at a time. Nobody could recall afterwards that he had ever been into Henriette's nurseries, perhaps might have had to ask the house-keeper which of the rooms were being used for the purpose. As soon as Henriette was old enough to ask questions and retain the answers, she heard Guffy excusing her father. He was a good man, she said. It was not his fault, he had had no parents, he could not be expected to understand. 'Every time he sees you,' Guffy sighed, 'he misses your mother, poor soul, it makes him sad.' Her childhood, such as it was, slipped through his hands.

Henriette's heavy features, slightly over-grown, already angular, were very like her mother's. So was the colouring, especially the melancholy white of the skin. Her eyes were dark, but something of her father's determination was in the gaze.

The Alsatian governness, Mademoiselle Mechtilde, taught French, both spoken and written, elementary mathematics, the history of Louis XIV, her favourite period. Also where Guffy had delighted in the girl's appetite, the governess insisted on a diet. There came a day when Henriette was escorted down to the drawing-room, to recite Lafontaine fables. As a reward for the performance, Gustav sat her on his knee. The sight, the touch of her, brought watering into his eyes. Clinging to him, Henriette held her arms tight round his neck.

'I should have been mother and father to you.'

Break-through, storming the heights, the lifting of the siege; Henriette would recall the scene, as a general might, in military language.

True to his word, Gustav took charge of her upbringing. The violence of his reaction proved how he reproached himself for lost opportunity and wasted affection. The two of them became inseparable. As though she were his contemporary, he told her how at about her age he had so hated his circumstances that he had run away, lived on the road, stolen food to stay alive, forced his luck. (Once when Hannah Schlesinger took her to a tea-room, the nine-year-old Henriette offered to pay, with the words foreshadowing her adult self – 'You have already done more than enough for us.')

A stool was set up for her in the office downstairs, alongside Gustav and Margulies, for serious study over balance sheets and accounts. No doubt Gustav was training her to take his place. What he had achieved, she would hold and improve. The two of them were creators. Never sell, Gustav taught, there's no stopping it, break the spiral, select what to buy instead. The destroyers, the stupid, were not to be blamed, merely avoided. Make, build, grow, multiply. The purpose of money was use, not accumulation, and those who understood that were free spirits. To such as them, money was a medium, like water to a fish or air to an animal.

The year of Henriette's tenth birthday also saw the celebration of the first twenty years of Concordia. To her, there was mystical significance in being, for this one unrepeatable moment, half the factory's age. Before the ceremony, a room was arranged for her in Gustav's former quarters, and there she slept on a hard narrow bed. Looking out of the windows she saw flames against the night sky, the shadows of men moving about their work. The roar and confusion of the factory excited her.

31

In the courtyard a marquee had been erected for speeches, then a dinner. And she was going to speak from the platform, to propose congratulations, and wish a long and successful future to what one day would be hers. She memorised what Gustav had written for her : 'Concordia has been, is, and will be always a name for each of us to carry in our heart.' At her father's side she did not feel nervous, not even when the minister, Chlumecky, arrived, with a number of officials from his ministry; not even when she stood on the platform with Solkovsky and Eduard von Arnheim. Her cue arrived, she was word-perfect. A week later, a certificate of merit, made out to her and signed by Chlumecky, was delivered by messenger.

In that same autumn of 1901, the Ellingen Waisenhaus was opened. The building acquired for the purposes was on the corner of the Dornbacherstrasse, in the Favoriten slums. Thirty Jewish children were to be cared for, boys and girls alike, in a place from which none of them would wish to run away.

'We orphans have one advantage,' Gustav said in his address (printed at his expense, and somewhat conventional it is too), 'that we are obliged to look after ourselves, and to develop endurance and thrift. Without courage, however, nothing can be achieved.' Professional training was to be provided. By the outbreak of the First War, the orphanage was taking pride in the number of doctors and nurses graduating from its ranks.

'Since you care for the children of our people,' the Oberrabbiner of Vienna asked at that opening of the orphanage, 'why are you refusing to raise your own Henriette in a Jewish house ?'

Gustav quoted himself – *'Jude muss man sein aber nicht zum Abattoir.'*

'You are not asked to go to the slaughterhouse, but to bring your child up according to our faith and our traditions.'

The Oberrabbiner was elderly, his voice had complaint rising through it. Moreover, he had felt free to place a hand around Henriette's shoulders while speaking about her. To

Henriette, the Oberrabbiner's clothes had a stiff, musty smell, his beard disappeared at the neck like a ragged scarf, that hand felt dead.

·Seven·

No sooner had Gustav become a baron than he ordered complete sets of glasses with a capital E and a coronet engraved on them. When the crates were delivered, the servants spent an entire day unpacking them. More glasses had been bought than could be arranged in cupboards, and the surplus was repacked into crates and deposited in the cellars. Household linen had also to be suitably monogrammed; silver trays and salvers too, serving-dishes, forks and spoons in baize-lined boxes. Telling Leviseur or Fräulein Lindner that he required a dozen of something, he meant a dozen dozen. On envelopes, even from abroad, the three words 'Baron Ellingen, Vienna' were enough for the postman.

Novelty had its daily rhythm, acquisition its magic. In Henriette's mind, it was never in doubt that everything was done for her as much as for her father. Companions of her own age were secondary to the company of this overwhelming man: that surely was the meaning of love, of her adoration. She copied his manner, studied herself in the mirror for resemblances. How she admired the way he set about achieving his ends.

At Sagodvar, Istvan Balogh the trainer, had said that Kismet was a stallion bred to hold his own anywhere, without a rival.

Gustav had replied, 'Let's win the Derby with him, then.'

Preparations lasted for two years. For the 1905 Derby, the horse was transported by train to Vienna. Henriette was at the station. Released from its stall, Kismet had reared, eyes rolling, prancing before ringing its hoofs down. 'Too nervous, a bad omen,' Balogh said.

In the week leading to the race, tensions tight as cramp

formed in Henriette's chest. Every afternoon, she and Guffy and Mademoiselle Mechtilde visited Kismet in the stalls at Freudenau, off the race-course. Balogh slept there, and so did the grooms, and Carstairs, the jockey, a man with broken front teeth. Too excited to sleep at night, she turned on the pillows, listening to the pulse of her heart. On the morning of the race, she awoke Guffy, who boiled her some milk, and they sat in the nursery by the open window as the summer sky began to lighten, picking out the trees in the park, lifting the surface of the lake to the palest blue. Eventually the maids brought up breakfast. A white piqué dress had been specially ordered, with a wide lace collar, and a hat to go with it, its trimmings of feathers – the first more or less grown-up hat she had worn.

Her father was dipping a croissant into his coffee when she knocked at his door. Even today he was going to wear his bowler-hat.

'If Kismet wins, everyone is going to know you're the owner.'

'We needed rain last week, the ground may be too dry for him.'

'Carstairs says to keep my eyes fixed on his gold cap.'

Rubbing at the top of his head, Gustav was amused. He said, 'I've forbidden Carstairs, all of them in fact, from placing a bet.'

In the hall, friends and the servants had assembled, and they broke into clapping as Gustav and Henriette walked downstairs. Solkovsky had brought his son Paul, aged four, and dressed in a uniform designed for the child, complete with buttons down the front of the tunic, miniature epaulettes and sword-belt.

At Freudenau, they watched Kismet being saddled. Groomed until the final moments, the horse had the sheen of polished mahogany. After the weigh-in, they went to places reserved in the Jockey Club stand. Gustav carried his heavy field-glasses, Henriette a pair covered in mother-of-pearl. On her right was Solkovsky, a cigar in his mouth, with his son standing on a seat.

35

The horses were under starter's orders when Henriette caught voices speaking behind her.

'Have you ever seen such a fright as that little Ellingen girl?'

'Straight from the ghetto.'

'Marry for money, and repent at the Wailing Wall.'

Four men in dress uniform were there, and one of the group was Sandor von Pechy, a military figure, stroking his moustache with the tip of a finger. Which of the four had said what was beyond her guessing. Apparently neither her father nor Solkovsky had heard the remarks. Under the shock of it, she did not concentrate on the start of the race, and before she was aware of it, the horses had passed in front of her, and were out of immediate sight. So that's what they think among themselves – the insight cut deep, a mortal wound.

The horses came round into the straight, and still she had failed to catch up on the advice not to let the gold cap out of her sight. So she missed how Carstairs brought Kismet through the centre of the field in a surge of speed, pulling out to the front, clearing away fast from the others. Those who were present at that race agreed that this finish was truly magnificent. For instance, Oberst Karl-Hans Jansch, manager of the Imperial stud at Napajedle, in his definitive history of breeding and racing in Austro-Hungary, comments that he had never seen a horse go more strongly than Kismet, nor a jockey more able to get the best out of a horse than Carstairs. For him, the Derby of 1905 had been the experience of a lifetime.

On all sides Gustav was congratulated. From the row behind, Sandor von Pechy and his brother-officers leant forward to shake his hand, applauding along with everyone else. Henriette could not help herself, she backed away as her father moved through the crowds to join Kismet and lead the horse in. In his delight, there and then he promised Carstairs that he could have the prize-money, as compensation for the bet he had not been permitted to place, '... thereby making a rich man of the jockey,' notes Jansch with disapproval, 'a precedent not adopted by other owners.'

The chance was lost for Henriette to be presented in the Imperial Box, curtsy to the Emperor, receive the trophy from his hands.

·Eight·

Another threshold into the grown-up world was crossed when Henriette moved downstairs into the room in which she had been born, where her mother had died. Maids carried down dresses and shoes and hats, her books including the complete *Bibliothèque Rose* which was the gift of Mademoiselle Mechtilde, the jewel-case with a locket holding a miniature of herself as well as assorted tie-pins and hat-pins and gold bracelets bought for her on each birthday by Gustav as though it were a tradition, silver-framed photographs of Kismet and the factory, a crocodile-skin writing-case with shagreen lining and a vanity-case to match, a mirror with a surround of lilies in *Jugendstil* coloured glass.

The purpose of the change, according to Gustav, was that the two of them should breakfast together, in his dressing-room, with the day's business off to a good start. She was also to attend his dinner-parties, receive his guests, act as the lady of the house. These names are taken at random from his address book, in itself a pocket *Who's Who* of Viennese society as it then was, Frau Geheimrat Dohme, Dr and Frau Dillel, Baron Doczy de Kermet-Kereszlar, Baron Richard Drasche von Wartinburg, Herr Anton and Herr Eugen Dreher, both of Schloss Kettenhof, Konstantin Dumba and Nikolaus Dumba, Sir Frederick and Lady Duncan of the British Embassy, Count Draskovich, Frau Hermine Delis, and so on. On the page facing the lists of names, Leviseur had noted not only addresses but correct titles, all in purple ink and a clerk's copper-plate hand.

In this society Gustav met Countess Marina Revertella (née Gradenigo). It was for her that Gustav once more retained his suite at the Imperial Hotel. Already turned sixty when he came to depend on Mimi, he had looked old for most of his life, largely on account of his baldness and his greed. Like Else, Mimi stood a head taller than him. When they were together, at least in public, she gave an impression of caring for him as for some demanding and unusual pet. Accordingly he behaved as though in need of a rug over his knees, someone to fuss with overcoat and hat and gloves, a helping hand to climb stairs. The affair was common knowledge.

A northern Italian family loyal to the Habsburgs, the Revertellas lived in Vienna and owned a palazzo in Venice. Mimi's husband, Ferdinand, was reputed to be one of the finest shots in Europe, to be mentioned along with Lord Ripon in England or the Duque de Suenca in Spain. He and his sportsmen friends staked out the calendar according to the kill for the season, chamois in the Alps, pheasants in England, big game in Africa. It was considered an honour that Ferdy accepted invitations to shoot partridges at Sagodvar.

The portrait by Sargent of Mimi at Marienbad, which is now in the Cleveland Museum, is dated 1906. She and Gustav had spent the summer there together, ostensibly for the cure. The probability is that Gustav commissioned and paid for the picture. Mimi is shown full-length, in a pose which reveals the long straight back and the turn of a beautiful neck. (And who paid for the diamonds on a ribbon of black velvet around that neck?) Auburn hair has been elaborately gathered up; the eyes are light brown, and very open; the expression is that of a woman rightly confident of pleasing. Sunshine illuminates the background, and a folded silk parasol completes a femininity which Sargent invites us to admire.

That same summer, Henriette was despatched with Guffy to Scotland, for four healthy weeks of sea-bathing at North Berwick. Not until September was she at Sagodvar, under the same roof as Mimi and Ferdy Revertella.

She could not wait to ask her father who this woman was. She had been at Marienbad with him, hadn't she?

'Mimi makes me a good companion. She's delicate, and she's lonely. Ferdy is away so much of the time.'

Would Mimi always send her into exile? Take over in her

39

own home? Henriette asked, 'What have I done to deserve this?'

'If she were a man she'd be capable of running the factory.'

In her own room, Henriette locked the door, lay on the bed, to sob loud enough to be sure to be overheard. She swore loyalty to the mother she had never known. Behind the locked door, she went to bed without food, and the whole household was involved in the hysteria.

Nothing speaks so well of Mimi as the way she succeeded in winning over a prickly fourteen-year-old with an in-built longing to be victimised, to suffer unjustly for the sins of others.

'I don't care for shooting, I refuse to ride, and tennis is boring. The neighbours are even more boring, so you and I must make the best of it.'

Mimi did nothing much more than spend time with Henriette, reading aloud, teaching her patiences and chess. Instead of solitary exhibitionistic sobbing, there was a sudden conspiratorial unity between two women equally jealous over an old man.

In the autumn, after the return to Vienna, Mimi continued to play her hand skilfully by staying away from Pernsdorf.

'Why does she never come here?' Henriette now asked her father.

'Because it wouldn't look right.'

'If I'm here, and I invite her, it would.'

Sometimes Mimi took her shopping, buying clothes for her which Guffy or Mademoiselle Mechtide would never have permitted, escorting her to doctor and dentist. At Christmas, Gustav and Henriette stayed with the Revertellas in Venice. A gondolier in livery took them to the house on Cà Foscari. For several days there was an unforgettable winter sun, with no warmth in it, but whose hard sparkle silvered the lagoon. In that light, each roof and facade was thrown into relief, as were the snow-capped mountains away on the mainland.

And as they were walking across a piazza on a morning's sightseeing, Mimi turned to Henriette, 'When I was your age, I dreamed all day long about love. What kind of a husband would you choose?'

'One like Ferdy.'

The answer had been given without reflection. Henriette could not have explained why it was a victory, nor what sort of victory it might be to match Mimi's cleverness unexpectedly. Neither was in any danger from the other.

The following summer, Gustav took the cure at Marienbad once more, and the year after that at Bad Nauheim, which then became his favourite spa. On the same floor of the hotel, he engaged rooms not only for himself and Mimi, but for Henriette and Guffy and the governess. Marietta and Toni, the Revertella children, born in 1908 and 1910 respectively, could either or both have been Gustav's.

·*Nine*·

For Henriette's eighteenth birthday, the share-holding of Concordia was restructured. In the new issue, the major holding was Gustav's – 27,089 shares to be precise – but he handed them over to Henriette, retaining only the life-interest. Prince Solkovsky acquired 7,900. To Ferdy Revertella were allocated 3,113 shares, in return for which he never attended a single meeting, and it may be presumed that he did not bother with anything except the annual dividend-coupon. Eduard von Arnheim and his son had ninety-nine shares apiece, while two other directors, Dr Loebel and Dr Johann Verelst, each had five. Quite why there should have been 38,410 shares in all must reflect some boardroom consideration long since forgotten.

31 March 1909 was overcast, but mild, at the end of a spiteful winter. As a precaution against a relapse of the weather, a tent had been erected at Pernsdorf between the house and the lake. Chairs had been arranged alongside, in the open on the lawn, on stands to accommodate four rising rows. In the background was the ancient copper-beech, finest of the trees in the park, at least forty foot in girth.

An heiress was coming into her own. Towards midday Gustav took his seat in the centre of the front row. He was wearing a frock-coat and top hat. For the commemorative photograph the posture he adopted was unsmiling, challenging, the legs pushed apart by his weight, hands resting on his knees. On his right was Henriette, standing up and leaning over in confidence, her arm around his shoulders, her hat with its wide brim seeming to brush against him. On her other side sat Prince Solkovsky, also in frock-coat and top hat, bulky and bearded, in a model of royalty. Two of a kind, heraldic supporters as it were, flanked Henriette. Behind her, as though in feminine solidarity, were Miss Magoffin, Mademoiselle Mechtilde and Fräulein Lindner, in blacks and greys more appropriate to a funeral. The only other woman in this gathering of over a hundred men was Frau Gitta Osterset-zer, wife of the head of the Waisenhaus.

Occupying other front-row chairs were the von Arnheims, the directors of Concordia and subsidiary companies, Egyedy the bailiff from Sagodvar, and Balogh the stud trainer. Also Margulies, his face behind a pair of gold-rimmed spectacles apparently too tight, an instrument for self-punishment. In the rows behind, in order of precedence, were lesser managers and executives, rising on the top benches at the rear to Hungarian employees, foresters and head-keepers in local costume, with plumes and feathers in their hats. To one side, next to a seated Dr Ostersetzer, had been shepherded a flock of owl-eyed children from the orphanage, buttoned into page-boy uniforms.

Lunch was laid at tables in the tent. On behalf of the guests, Prince Solkovsky presented Henriette with a silver tray on which were inscribed the names of those present, excluding the last row and the orphans. Their names (the orphans again excepted) were also recorded on the lower margin of the photograph finally given to her. The great proportion of these men in the service of her father were Jews. In that respectful, deferential, group there stood out a single figure in the second row, sideways on to the camera, with a white silk scarf non-chalantly round his throat, his top hat shining and rakish. He can be identified as Isidor Schneidersohn. Whether or not this Schneidersohn intended his smile to be mocking or sarcastic is now as uncertain as the exact role he fulfilled once in the hierarchy of the Ellingen empire.

Gustav's advice was, 'You may do with the Concordia shares whatever you like, so long as you keep them. For us, the factory holds the place of family, we have no other re-lations. It'll look after us. Is steel consumption likely to drop in your life-time ? Solkovsky is right, those with shares in this business will never have to sleep on straw.'

Attendance at Concordia board-meetings became obligatory. She took naturally to production charts, labour costs, investment projections, sensing the surge of power in numerals across the pages. She had an instinct: she liked or did not like the look of a thing, the feel of it. It was a proper upbringing, Gustav said, unlike his.

At the same time, she also inherited from her grandfather. In his will Professor Theodor Dreinach had written, 'I leave all such means as I have to Henriette, in the hopes of fulfilling the promise of her dear mother, my only child, whose lineaments I have always been so touched to see in her.'

Like a leaf in winter, in Gustav's expression, the old man had outlived his purposes. Together with Henriette, he paid the house a final visit, and instructed the packers. Soon afterwards, builders moved in and converted the premises into offices, which were let as the headquarters of an insurance company. Henriette received the income, and another ledger was opened for her by Margulies.

The projected history of folk migrations in the Dark Ages was transferred to Pernsdorf, where a room under the roof was made available to house the entire deposit. Dozens of cardboard boxes, a series of files with complex numberings, thousands of reference cards, duly indexed, in wooden boxes. Several hand-written manuscripts existed, including annotations in red and in green ink. Each version differed, with chapters added or deleted. Some passages had been left incomplete, or on the contrary were in parallel but inconsistent drafts.

A university colleague, Professor Pollner, wrote for permission to work on this material. The book, in his opinion, could be prepared for the press within a year. Nor was this a labour of love, but nothing less than what was due to a great scholar, an authority. New light was cast here on the origins of nations, on why some peoples had become civilised, others had vanished from history. His own teaching commitments, however, reduced the time Professor Pollner could spend among the Dreinach papers. For a while he came to lunch on a Wednesday, and shut himself away for an afternoon's research in the room upstairs. Then he delegated the task of sifting and comparing the alternative manuscripts to a doctoral student of his. Asked when the text might be concluded, this man answered, 'Very soon.' But he had trouble with his eyes, complained of the strain, and 'Dr Very Soon', as he had been nicknamed, in his turn withdrew into the university, and the Dreinach archive lay untouched.

·Ten·

At one of Bijou Landau's parties, Henriette noticed a man noticing her. His skin was exceptionally sallow, as though never exposed to fresh air. The hair, light in texture, was strong; he would not go bald. Nor would he become fat: a compact figure, with the elegance of absolute self-control, no gesture too emphatic. She overheard him speaking fluent French and English.

Rudolf Hechter was a banker. Already turned thirty.

'He knows what he wants,' Bijou Landau said. To which she added, 'They're the ones you feel sorry for.'

Her husband Horace Landau collected odd verses and epigrams, which he published at his own expense in limited editions for his friends.

'The parents are rich by any standards,' he said. 'Suppliers of medical equipment. That young man is certain to make his mark.'

Introduced to Rudolf, Henriette observed how his lips naturally formed into a smile, as though there were a joke, or at least irony, just below the surface of everything. His eyelashes were curved, more like a woman's. On the little finger of his left hand was a signet-ring.

Soon Rudolf was calling regularly at Pernsdorf. He sat for hours over cups of tea with Gustav (who was suspicious of affectation and said to Henriette, 'Ask if there's a stethoscope on that ring of his.').

Briefe, Die Ihn Nicht Erreichen was a famous book at the time, consisting of letters which were designed to alleviate awkward circumstances, but actually provoked disaster. Rather in parody of the book's style, Henriette wrote such a letter to Rudi, anonymously and in English: a declaration of love.

46

When next he was at Pernsdorf, she led him into the library. He examined a number of books on the shelves.

'Your father has very wide interests.'

'Nebenzahl the dealer has been sending him all the right titles for years.'

'You shouldn't write in English, you know, your spelling is atrocious. Miss Magoffin should be shot.'

'What did I get wrong?'

'Passion, unlike fashion, has no *h* in it. And as for your spelling of idolize...'

'What should it be?'

'R, l, b, f, p – English, I expect you know, is not phonetic. You deserve a confession from me. I have a secret vice, namely my Jewish nerves. I'm a creature of habit, and it is a vice to be so thoroughly afraid of the future as I am.'

What could the future bring except more of the same, the luxuries of Pernsdorf and Sagodvar, boundless years of Derby winners, columns of figures in purple ink down the right-hand margins of ledgers? After his departure, she wrote him a series of letters, signed now, to ask what he had meant. On a single sheet of paper, he eventually replied that she should now try the French language, so notable for its clarity.

Gustav said, 'He's after your money, and he'd be a fool not to chase it.'

And another caution, 'Nobody in the banks seems to have much to say about this fellow. All he does every day is walk up and down the Kärntnerstrasse.'

All the same, he checked on the state of the market for medical supplies, and he travelled to the house in the country where the Hechter parents lived.

Invited to Sagodvar in August 1913, Rudolf accepted. As a shot he was well able to hold his own, even though at the end of a long hot day his face had no sign of a flush.

'The reason I couldn't marry you,' Rudolf said, 'is that everybody would accuse me of doing it for the money.'

'You aren't exactly poor yourself.'

'Your father is overwhelming.'

'Marry for money, repent at the Wailing Wall.'

Listening to her explanation of this, he twitched his lips into the thinnest smile.

'Perhaps our forebears knew best when they left these things to marriage-brokers.'

And then he asked, 'You seem to have been brought up to know nobody except the nanny who can't spell and a father who treats you like a contemporary of his. Don't you have any friends?'

'You have enough for both of us.'

No more formal a proposal followed. In the autumn of 1913, he went on what he called leave, like a soldier. From Paris and London letters arrived about people and places, concerts, ballets, museums. In reply, Henriette depicted the state of her soul.

Instinct. The avoidance of stupidity in others. Rudolf was far from stupid but he was the first more or less suitable man to have presented himself. Greater expertise would have been applied to the purchase of a new share. Not once did she question the rightness of the choice, and certainly not when, on 30 June 1914, she stood under the canopy in the Seitenstettengasse synagogue, where Gustav and Else had been married before her.

For the honeymoon, Rudolf had rented a house on the Starnbergersee, but he grew restless in the placid scenery of Bavaria, and they moved up to Berlin, where he knew Liebermann, Paul Cassirer, Kühlmann the former foreign minister, the Friedländer-Fulds, Goldschmidt, the sculptor Guarini with a studio at Jäckelsbruck. Henriette was a bride of hardly five weeks standing when this social life came to a halt, and on a sunny day she found herself standing at the hotel window for a view of the crowds surging and cheering in the streets below, with war-fever on them.

·*Eleven*·

War was declared as Gustav reached Bad Nauheim. There could be no question of Mimi joining him. By telegram he ordered Henriette and Rudolf home. An echo of the long-ago past was carried in the unexpected and solitary journey to Vienna. At Pernsdorf the lodge-gates were closed. A startled porter put his head into the back of the car to be sure that this really was Baron Gustav returning. Not since the house had been built had Gustav been there in August, to see for himself how the grass withered in the park under the heat, how airless the shuttered rooms became. In his absence, dust-sheets covered the furniture, the curtains had been taken down. The servants were away, and it was not possible to remedy these things. Upstairs, Miss Magoffin was recovering from a summer cold. She prepared a meal, and the two of them ate at the kitchen table, which was without precedent.

'My responsibilities are here,' Miss Magoffin said. 'I shall stay with Henriette.'

'You will do nothing of the kind.'

Miss Magoffin packed her trunk, and while she was about to close it, Gustav scattered in among her folded possessions a number of sovereigns. 'If anyone asks,' he said, 'you say that they were in a bag but must have fallen out.' Escorting her himself to the station, he said goodbye under the eyes of a panicky attaché who was trying to correlate the names on his lists. Then he had himself driven to the Imperial Hotel where he ordered for himself alone a double dinner.

Those grey eyes were cold and blank whenever anyone asked what he predicted, or what ought to be done for the best. The thoughts were secret but the actions spoke for themselves : he settled into the library, hitherto not a room he had used. 'My father-in-law prepared this for me,' he said, 'and now my son-in-law will tell me how to take advantage of it.' He liked to discuss what he had been learning and discovering: this Spinoza, more gloomy than he need have been, Voltaire a Jew-hater and a misery, Balzac always sound on money. In the afternoons he fell asleep, the books slipping from his lap. A year into the war, and he ceased dressing properly, neither buttoning his shirt on to its stud nor putting on a collar, wrapping himself into a house-coat with velvet facings. Burschen Franz served him his meals in the library on a card-table laid with a Turkish rug. Except on the hottest days, the fire was lit.

'You must not let yourself go,' an angry Solkovsky argued with him. 'Today Concordia needs you more than ever. The Minister keeps asking why you do not pull your weight. The war is going to last for a very long time, and the factory will be in a quite different position at the end of it.'

Gustav refused to be drawn; he stayed at home without explanation, rubbing at the top of his head, reading, staring out at the seasons changing in the park, immobilised in his thoughts.

'The trouble is,' Solkovsky complained to Henriette, 'that pipes and tubes have a way of becoming gun-barrels and gun-carriages. Experts are moving in, we really are in their hands. We need him to stand up for the factory. If the country were to fail, he'd fail with it. He will not face so unfamiliar a notion.'

Henriette answered, 'Other people's stupidities have become unavoidable. The war has made an old man out of him.'

'I'd rather say he's still never grown up.'

Drafted on to ministerial committees, privy to confidences from the government and the General Staff, Solkovsky was in his element, more politician at last than industrialist. Month after month, the Concordia production figures climbed.

Early in 1916 Henriette began to feel unwell. Nothing was wrong, Dr Kottlowicz assured her, only she was expecting a child. Lying in bed, she morbidly imagined herself to be about to complete the cycle begun by her mother. No mother's arms had held her, no mother's arms would hold her child, it would be another Ellingen orphan. Self-pity was succeeded by practicality. Under her instructions, the kitchen garden was enlarged and planted up to its full extent. Part of the stable block was converted to raise hens and guinea-fowl. Goats were tethered in the park.

On medical gronds, Rudolf had been rejected for active military service. Gazetted lieutenant, he had been appointed a translator in the Foreign Office, using his French and English to his heart's content. Something was wrong with every part of him, he said, from anaemia in the blood-stream to flat feet. The hours of work were too long, Pernsdorf too far away for him to be able to commute every day. Instead, he decided to rent rooms in the centre of the old city, within walking distance of the Ballhausplatz.

'The house is as empty as a tomb,' Henriette said. 'Nobody considers me. You sit in your office reading old copies of *The Times* and the *Figaro* as if you were in your club. A week might very well pass before you learn about the child, and whether I'm alive or dead.'

'I am working on the artillery manual concerning the improved 25-pounder, as a matter of fact. And the child, like every child, will come into the world unassisted by its father.'

'One must be prepared for the worst,' Henriette told Primarius Fleischmann when he moved into the house. 'Nothing can alter a destiny like mine.' 'The course of events is decided by nature,' he replied, 'with a helping hand from science, if you like.'

'Speaking of destiny,' he added, 'I can think of no child brought into the world under more fortunate auspices.'

Taking a period of leave, Rudi settled into the library, to wait on events in the company of Gustav. Until the small hours each night, the two men smoked cigars, played chess, drank brandy which had been laid down in the cellars in the year when the house was completed. In the afternoon of 2 November 1916, Primarius Fleischmann carried down to the library the newly born boy, to be inspected by his father and grandfather. To the midwife's horror, Gustav insisted on seeing the baby undressed, and to hell with the cold weather and the lack of heat from the fire.

'And what is the boy's destiny ?' Rudi asked.

About such things, about what might happen next in the war or the possibility of a political outcome, Gustav was silent. Distance, rather than pessimism, seemed to lie in his grey eyes. His pleasures were in his meals and his books, and in holding and cradling the grandson always called Jules, as though to show that even in war-time French affinities were natural.

Julius Hechter was one of the very last to be born to qualify as a citizen of Kaiser Franz Josef. That same month, the old emperor died.

Early in the new reign a letter was received from the Finance Ministry. An appointment with Gustav was requested. Two representatives from the Ministry called, both young men of an age when they might have been on active service. Gustav had dressed formally to receive them, but he did not rise from his chair when they entered the library.

'You may say what you wish in front of my daughter, and my advisor Margulies, they enjoy my full confidence.'

The two civil servants apologised for disturbing him, but their request was of national importance. However the course of the war might be determined, the coming peace had already to be anticipated.

Resources were to be mobilised, first and foremost, for the long-term protection of the currency. The example of patriotism was in order. The minister himself was appealing to the Baron to bring his fortune home from Switzerland.

Listening, Gustav as usual kept his opinions to himself. The men from the Ministry withdrew, their car could be heard outside on the drive.

'That means the war is quite definitely lost,' Margulies burst out. 'Next time we have visitors like that, they'll be speaking of mobilising total wealth. We shall see impositions, levies, outright confiscation, public theft.'

'And what might stabilisation mean ?'

'That we are supposed to join them in their folly. The rewards of a life-time are to be thrown to the winds. Think of your daughter and grand-son.'

Of course, Margulies continued, news of the Baron's refusal would be leaked to the press by the frustrated officials. Accusations of disloyalty were dangerous at a time like this, but less fatal than inability to finance industrial operations. A time was coming in this ruined country when the factory would be obliged to convert back to normal operations; in the event of defeat, perhaps to manufacture other products, according to the whim of the Allies. The Baron's responsibility was not to a dissolving empire, but to Concordia and its employees and their families. The public would never believe that such a figure-head as Baron Gustav had no capital, he had to remain solvent. And why the Ellingen fortune? No individual contribution could have the slightest impact on the national budget. This was victimisation. The story was familiar : the authorities, in a dilemma, had nothing better to do than pick on a Jew. Put another way, everyone had to be as incompetent and blind as the authorities. They had made the mess and then ensured that the Jews were in it.

In the event, Gustav did nothing. The weather became warmer, and on fine days Gustav had himself wheeled by Burschen Franz down to the lake. A dozen goats grazed there now, with their kids. And it was out of doors that pain seized his chest, he slumped forward, scraping the pink skin of his face on the side of his chair.

All that summer and autumn Gustav lay propped on pillows in bed. Under the monogrammed sheets, their edges trimmed with blue ribbon, his chest rose and fell as though the energy in him could not be discharged. That first stroke had paralysed his left side, and confused his speech. Any day he might go, Dr Kottlowicz said, and recovery was impossible.

More than one letter from the Ministry inquired what measures the Baron proposed, and Margulies replied that the Baron was no longer in a position to be bothered with such matters. Like detectives, the two officials insinuated themselves once more into the house, evidently sceptical.

The war was in its final year when, against all odds, Gustav improved. His speech clarified. The windows of his bedroom were thrown open for the scent of limes. Those wide grey eyes seemed to search far beyond the house, its park and lodge. Rudolf read newspapers aloud.

'Are they still badgering us ?' Gustav asked. 'Then send in Margulies.'

Not the entire fortune, Margulies prevaricated. Half a million, at most a million, would serve the purpose. Not all four million gold crowns. It was unthinkable. He did what he could to delay it, in Vienna, as in Zurich. Gustav himself drafted the instructions.

Solkovsky made the last appeal, a Solkovsky dejected at every prospect. Sitting on the edge of the bed, he held Gustav's hands, he rubbed them as though to comfort a child. It was time to keep everything away from the mob, he said, people like them risked being trampled to death. Murder would reign everywhere, as already in Russia. All that remained was to look after oneself.

'This country has been good to me, I'll settle accounts with it.'

A few weeks longer, and Margulies and Solkovsky might have succeeded, as the fronts disintegrated and the war faded into defeat. But Gustav had signed the order. All four million gold crowns. By the end of the year the money had been duly transferred into Austrian currency, at a season when leaves went swirling down the pavements, the scudding sky promised heavy snowfalls, and the young emperor drove away with his family and a few retainers from an abandoned palace, to close the dynasty. Armed men in a lorry did in fact push past the lodge-gates and circled the drive, but passed on from Pernsdorf before they could be identified. Four million gold crowns in support of an order which no longer existed, in a paper currency depreciating to lose all value, undoing the achievement of a life-time.

After his second stroke, Gustav seemed to retrace his past as he muttered to himself about running away 'with my back to the afternoon sun', about the man on the gibbet, Hannah, and

Max who had lost his money in '73. Under the sheets his chest heaved and fell, but more quietly. Henriette and Rudolf hardly knew how to fill in the time, opening cupboards for a sight of unworn suits in out-of-date styles, and stiff shirts still in pre-war cartons packed and posted in London, and box after box of Grimshaw's talcum powder. They brought in Jules to impress on the boy that he should remember his grandfather, only to push him off upstairs to spare his feelings. And the crowns, Baron Gustav mumbled more and more incoherently, Margulies will have to buy them back, if necessary at a premium, or have them covered, have them insured. Make, build, grow, multiply. Was it possible, they whispered in that house where the lights were never put out, to die of such things?

·Part Two·

·Twelve·

A studio portrait of Jules at the age of five shows him seated on a giant cushion, against a backdrop painted to represent creamy clouds. For the occasion he had been dressed in a white shirt with ruffles and a lace collar wide around the neck. Velvet trousers, fastened on two large nacreous buttons, stopped below the knee, to leave the shin bare, and to expose white socks above ankle-boots apparently in patent leather. His head of black curls had been elaborately brushed. High forehead, round chin, large eyes with girlish lashes like his father's. With one leg extended in front of him, the other tucked up underneath him on the cushion, he appears in the pose of a would-be potentate, if it were not for the look of far-away and utter self-absorption so often found in children who do not know what is expected of them. A more natural expression had been inhibited, if not forbidden, by the photographer (who signed his work *C.Pietzner, 'Künstlerische Ausführung von Photographien aller Arten'*).

In contrast, there are snapshots of Jules taken at about the same time, in the setting of Pernsdorf. For instance, on the lawn – where Burschen Franz carried out a table and laid on it a silver urn under which flickered a spirit lamp – Jules was the only child among his parents' guests, the women in ankle-length dresses and hats often in prewar styles and sizes, the men stiff-collared, in buttoned jackets. Or on his tricycle, its wheels of equal size and with ungainly rubber tyres, escorted by a groom as though on a pony. For him, Henriette's cart was brought out and revarnished, harnessed to goats no longer required for their milk but kept on for sentimental reasons. The lake was considered unsafe for paddling – mud and sediment, weeds, water-lilies – and so footmen fetched out a tin bath from the stables and filled it up at the water's edge, for Jules in a black bathing costume to splash about inside and to negotiate its slippery sides. Perhaps the boy imagined himself at play on his own, but in most of these photographs a straight-backed and serious Miss Magoffin is standing by.

Miss Magoffin had returned as though at the end of a lengthy and unwelcome vacation. Once again the nursery became a place apart from the rooms downstairs. On the walls were prints of stage-coaches. Trays were brought up the back-stairs by maids – Guffy's German after all these years was only good enough to tell the kitchen what she wanted. From the top of these stairs a corridor turned in a maze under the eaves and past the rooms in the turrets, up and down steps or narrow flights of smaller stairs, through a glass-enclosed tunnel with a view of the central dome, to return to the starting-point. A red-bordered fibre matting covered the entire course. Jules taught himself to run round and round this corridor, jumping at corners, sliding and scrambling, in private races of his own, with a record to beat. This was his favourite occupation, pushing himself to self-imposed limits, until he was so tired that he could only fall asleep.

'It's the shock of having to learn English with you,' Henriette told Guffy.

Then – 'I think he's upset by the death of his grandfather.'

'We can't mind about him running,' Miss Magoffin said, 'it's just high spirits.'

Nobody was able to coax an explanation out of the boy. His feet could be heard drumming and pounding round the corridor, and round once more, disturbing the peace. When they spoke about it, or threatened punishment, Jules fell silent, staring down the grown-ups. Released, he could not wait to resume his racing.

Nightmares began. Twisting and shivering in his sleep, the boy screamed. Shaken awake, he had nothing to confide, crying into his pillow.

The most famous child specialist in Vienna was Professor Warschawsky, of the Universitätsklinik. His consulting rooms were as spacious as *salons*, with a set of tapestries covering the walls. The professor had a bass voice, and spoke from a great height. He gripped the boy's arms.

'And what is your name, Jules ?'

Since he evidently knew, why tell him ?

Two consultations followed, and the professor then sent for Henriette and Rudolf. He spoke in front of Jules.

'There is no impediment, we need not be anxious. This child does not talk to us because he does not want to. And when he does want to, he will. He is a fine little fellow.'

Opening a drawer, he picked out some orange sweets for the boy. In the car on the way home, Henriette and Rudolf questioned their son, in the expectation that this session with the specialist was the prelude to a cure : there would be no more frenzied running in the corridor, no further unexplained nightmares. Jules stayed completely silent, as if deprived of the power of speech. Several days later, Przeweck, the new chauffeur, found the orange sweets under the arm-rest of the rear-seat, where they had crushed together and congealed.

·*Thirteen*·

Even in the earliest years of marriage, during the war, Rudolf had brought home a carpet, a *bergère*, some porcelain, Chinese bronzes. Sales and auctions, he said, were his hobby, and never before had they been so frequent or so advantageous. Beautiful objects would share the fate of their owners and become war-casualties unless someone like him came to the rescue. But then something else had to be displaced to make room for these purchases. The house, and everything in it, was a tribute to Gustav. What had been good enough for her father was good enough for Henriette. Change was upsetting, disrespectful to the spirit, with Gustav so recently dead and buried. Yes, the house was a perfect period piece, Rudolf conceded, but still he knew what he was doing.

A place on the main staircase above the Lecomte-de-Nouy could accommodate a formal conversation piece by Moritz von Schwind, and it was sent round on approval. The picture showed the Essler family, a lawyer and his wife and children, picknicking on a hill within sight of their native Salzburg. 'These people are too dreary to be invading my privacy,' Henriette said, 'I don't want to exchange glances with them every time I go up to bed.'

'The measurements just allow me to hang it in my office, if I can get it past the landing.'

'Office? You were a banker.'

'I've hung up one uniform, I'm not about to wear another.' Banking bored him, he said. The making of money was an activity best left to those who needed to do so. A van removed the Moritz von Schwind to the Michaelerplatz, where it was able to squeeze a way round the landing and into his rooms. Evening clothes were also kept there permanently, so that he could change if he was going out to dine or to the theatre. As in the war, he might telephone at the last moment to say that he would be spending the night in his flat.

And then there was Jacques Chauzal, a junior officer attached to the French military mission. Appointed after the war as one of the military attachés at the embassy, Chauzal had a car and a flat, and privileges at a time of shortages and austerity.

'How old can he be?' Henriette asked, when Rudolf first invited the man to Pernsdorf.

'Twenty-nine, I believe.'

'More like fifteen, with that baby-face, so pink and clean.'

'Civilised people rise above vulgar politics. The war wasn't our fault. I met Jacques long ago in Paris, very few men know so much about art. And he can open every door. Besides, he enjoys coming here for the billiard table.'

At home, Rudolf read for hours in the library, as Gustav had done towards the end of his life. With the intensity of a scholar rather than a dilettante, he absorbed Graetz, Dean Milman, Morison's *History of the Jews in the Roman Empire*, annotating margins and end-papers in a miniscule hand. Darwin and Wallace, Renan, Hacker, Fleg, and theological controversy in all forms fascinated him. So did the cranks and madmen, Gobineau, Lombroso, Toussenel, and Houston Stewart Chamberlain. And Drumont. Like a fly on fly-paper, he was held fast by animus against Jews. A shelf was devoted to publications about the Dreyfus case. Here, on his own, he fought the rear-guard action against those who would hate him for what he was. When he broke off, it was to go upstairs to the nursery to try to coax Jules into laughter, to interrupt the rhythm of the race round the upper corridor, to watch the boy eat.

Nobody can sit silent right through a meal, he used to say. Even hermits mumble.

'Who is the hermit under this roof?' Henriette asked, 'I have to do everything for myself.'

'That is your birth-right.'

'You must help. I want you on the board of Concordia.'

'Gentlemen are no good in those positions, you have only to look at Solkovsky. Why give myself airs? I'd bankrupt you.'

In the long months while Baron Gustav had lain dying, Solkovsky could do little or nothing. His intentions were voiced behind their backs. Both Margulies and Eduard von Arnheim warned Henriette in advance what to expect from Prince Solkovsky. No more the adventurer he had been, the man was diminished with defeatism. He was quoted as saying, 'Concordia and I were dancing when the others had already left the ball.' Geared into the war-effort, the factory, quite as much as the army, had to suffer the consequences of defeat. In the absence of orders, the work-force was being laid off; a new approach was required but modernisation would be prohibitively expensive. The blame lay between him and Gustav whose quixotic nature had finally got the better of him.

What I was trained to do, Henriette told herself, was to take decisions, to stand on my own feet, live up to a great man. It could not be helped. She summoned Solkovsky, the two of them lunched at Pernsdorf. He had lost weight. Nothing seemed to fit any more, neither his old-fashioned clothes nor his manners.

'The world as it is today must be faced,' Solkovsky said. 'I hope to spend what little is left of my life at Rentzenburg. I am making provisions for my poor Irina, and Paul. We find ourselves citizens of this Czechoslovakia all of a sudden, with our one asset this side of the border.'

He went on, 'Do you know, it is impossible to stop men creeping up the railway tracks to pilfer our coal-stocks at night? Concordia exists only in name.'

'What do you suggest?'

'Not all Gustav's gold has yet gone up the chimney.'

The choice was clear: either Henriette would have to buy out the minority share-holders, or else agree to sell with them. For weeks she went over the variable figures with Eduard von Arnheim, Margulies, directors and accountants, unable to decide what value to place on Concordia in present circumstances, nor how to express this value effectively with local currency inflating into meaningless millions and billions.

Almost as agitating to her as the future of the factory was Gustav's graveside memorial; as if the one could not be settled without the other, as if the man and all his works might vanish without trace and she would have become the orphan.

In the winter following Gustav's death, Rudolf and Henriette drove out to the Zentralfriedhof. It was early in the afternoon. The walk from the main gateway to the section reserved for Jews was a good fifteen minutes. Henriette felt her feet grow cold in light-soled shoes. Grey marble, it had been decided for the memorial, to be cut in solid blocks so that the joins hardly showed, tapering towards the top, a truncated pyramid. Halfway up, a bust of Gustav was to be fixed on to a plinth, with the name below in lettering of brass, without accompanying dates or his title. The masons needed final instructions about alignments.

'The scale, look at the scale.'

Always the connoisseur, Rudolf tilted his head, half-shutting his eyes, 'This is the kind of thing butchers erect in country villages.'

'It's as we knew it would be. You liked the drawings, you approved them.'

'I was wrong, then. What would the dear old man have said at the false heroism of this? That bust too. We shall have to slim the whole horrible thing down, it can't be helped, it's too ugly.'

Anger, like a rocket, fired in her. At such moments, black circles deepened in depression underneath her eyes.

'Why should his monument be smaller than the Guttmanns here, or the Manfred Weisses, or Baron Uhlmann?'

He looked astonished. 'Achievements are not measured like that.'

Listening to them, the foreman of the masons wiped his forehead with the back of his hand. Interpreting the gesture, Henriette said to him, 'You may proceed, it is exactly as I intended. If the bust seems to look to the right, then it is because that is the direction of Pernsdorf.'

That evening, as though to clarify a point and deflect anger,

Rudolf read aloud a passage from a book. 'In less than twenty years, if circumstances are favourable, the Jew attains his full development; he is born in the depths of some *Judengasse*, he earns a few sous in some preliminary operation, he opens up in Paris, he has himself discovered by means of some Dreyfus or other, buys the title of baron, presents himself boldly in society, taking on the airs of someone who has been rich all along. In such cases, transformation is in some way instantaneous, he feels no surprise, he is not even aware of certain reticences.'

'Am I supposed to recognise my father ?'

'It's Drumont's *La France Juive*. Showing that what really lies between us and anti-semites so often comes down to taste.'

Certain reticences. Marry for money, repent at the Wailing Wall. Taste, if that was what it was, had not affected Baron Gustav, had not been any sort of consideration. Make, build, grow, multiply. If only she listened, it seemed to her, her father's confident voice could be heard, and she would know what ought to be done.

Early in the new year, the crucial Concordia board-meeting was arranged. She told Rudolf to enter it into his diary.

'Indeed not' – he was at his most off-hand – 'Jacques has unearthed a Van Dyck drawing which may be for sale, and we are going to inspect it.'

'I am a woman, and not yet thirty. You have had the experience of a banker.'

'Be realistic. I have no right to attend, I'm not a shareholder, the others would perfectly properly object.'

The argument was always the same. If they were to share their lives successfully, it had to be in such a way that he owed her nothing. There was no point of leverage over him except money, and as he escaped from it, she cried with self-pity and rage.

But on the morning of the board-room meeting, he was waiting for her in the hall, took her hand and kissed it, led her out to the car, called after her in English, 'Good luck to you.'

Chill rain was falling. On hundreds of occasions she had

done this journey with her father, and every tree and house was familiar. The sprawl of the city now spread out to the factory, and into the farm-land beyond. Empty flat-cars stood in the sidings alongside the surrounding wall of the factory. Przeweck drove her across the yard to the offices, on whose steps Solkovsky and the others were clustered under umbrellas. The von Arnheims, representatives from the Credit-Anstalt and the Länderbank, Loebel and Verelst, the lawyer acting for Ferdy Revertella, like so many under-takers.

A greenish felt lined the passage leading to the board-room. Between its windows hung an enlarged photograph of the minister Chlumecky, Baron Gustav and herself on the podium for the twentieth anniversary of the factory. Glass-fronted bookcases contained unbroken rows of leather-bound volumes recording railway transactions right back to Gustav's early days. A cloth of a darker felt, discoloured with age, covered the board-room table. Gustav's chair, in oak, with its back and arms carved in German Gothic style, was twice the size of the other chairs, and on the wall behind it was a steel plate with Concordia stamped in relief.

To save money, the building was unheated, but close to the enormous oak seat stood a paraffin stove. The men round the table were looking to Henriette. She heard herself saying to them that her father's patriotism in a time of crisis had given Concordia a moral credit. Nobody could accuse her father of looking after his own interests first, or of profiteering. His voice came to her, saying, 'You may do with the Concordia shares whatever you like, so long as you keep them.' The factory would have to be recapitalised. Something might be salvaged from the repatriated gold crowns. Her race-horses would be sold, and so would the house of her Dreinach grand-parents. Bankers would do the rest. Any minority share-holder who so wished had only to sell her his holding.

At the end of the speech, the men around the table broke into applause. She was trembling with emotion. In a tone somewhere between a question and a statement, Solkovsky was first to speak.

'At pre-war prices ?'

'That will be settled privately.'

Withdrawing, she climbed the stairs to Gustav's bachelor quarters in the dizzying days of his early career. The rooms were unbearably damp, without any touch of life.

Margulies came to tell her that they must proceed with the agenda.

'There was no real choice,' he said, unexpectedly adding, 'And it may no longer matter, in these times.'

According to custom, lights were on throughout the house when she arrived home. A fire had been lit in her room. After a bath, she settled in bed against two square pillows. Anxiety had made her ravenous. As Gustav would have done, she wanted roast meat to devour, as much as possible.

Rain, heavier in the evening, slashed the windows. On the bedside table was the miniature in its carved frame which Else had given Gustav for their engagement. Also a horseshoe taken from Kismet after the race, and mounted in silver. Gustav's seal with his initials. One of her lacquer boxes, in which was a pressed four-leaf clover found by Rudolf during an early visit to Pernsdorf. Each and every object had associations and meanings too complex for words: addressed, as in prayer, these things interceded on her behalf. What might have been living experiences became tradition. Possessors of money were themselves possessed by it.

Amelie took away the empty plates of the meal, brought another pillow. The memorandum of the day's events and decisions had to be written. Then, in the dark, she watched the flickering fire which pulled shadows across the ceiling. Concordia – the syllables beat in the brain like the wheels of a train, the hoofs of a horse. What heritage would be left for the child upstairs in the grip of his fantasies? Towards two in the morning, a car could be heard on the drive. Rudi at last. She judged how long it would take him to make his way across the hall, up the curve of the staircase, to the door of his bedroom opposite. She surprised him. There he stood, in evening clothes.

'I haven't been able to sleep, I caught bronchitis today, they can't even warm the place. Here is what happened. I've put it down on paper.'

'Look at your spelling,' he said. 'F,q,w,r,a,d, what can the word be ?'

The pouches bulged under her eyes.

'No Van Dyck, not even a competent forgery. Our whole day was an utter waste of time.'

'We shall have to live very differently from now on. To save the factory, I have ruined myself.'

He took out his wallet and folded her sheets of paper into it.

'I expect we'll find that being ruined will be much the same as being rich.'

·*Fourteen*·

The Waisenhaus dominated its somewhat dingy end of the Dornbacherstrasse. Amid sooty buildings, it had a grey stucco exterior, an upright slab of a facade sliced by unusually elongated windows, the woodwork painted a constraining brown. In the adjoining garden or playground were laburnums, wispy and at a slant as though the effort to grow straight could not be managed in such a location. The Ellingen Foundation for Jewish Children: the words, in old-fashioned capitals, had been carved on a stone lintel inset above the entrance-porch, itself wooden and kennel-like. Under the terms of Baron Gustav's endowment, the children were to receive a Jewish education and upbringing. For them, he expected observances and pieties ignored or dismissed where he and his own family were concerned, a kosher kitchen, Hebrew, study of the Torah.

Endurance and thrift: the words were recycled at prize-givings or in addresses and speeches celebrating high holidays, Succoth, Purim, Hanukkah. On such occasions the children sang, recited, said prayers. Representatives from other institutions, and rabbis, governors, honorary vice-presidents including Rudolf's father, were present. The orphanage had long since been absorbed into the network of Jewish communal charities.

These children are not like you, Jules was told, they are unfortunate, to be pitied – if grandfather Gustav had not been so brilliant, you might very well have been one of them. Be on your best behaviour. A good boy does not keep his hands in his pockets. Eat whatever is put before you. In particular show respect to Dr Ostersetzer and his wife, who are there to pay the closest attention to everything that takes place.

On the day of the Waisenhaus piano performance, they set off from Pernsdorf in two cars, bringing among other guests Louise von Arnheim and Jacques Chauzal. The torments of the damned, Rudolf used to say, are bearable in the company of friends. The other children, it was thought, would be good for Jules, at least none of them raced round and round a corridor. For the occasion he was put into a white coat, its lining in the fleeciest of angora. He was seven.

A lady had been engaged to give the concert. Among her opening pieces were several Schubert dances, followed by a Mozart sonatina. During a break, the children were supposed to go into the dining-hall for their tea. Jules slipped to the piano, adjusted the seat, and began playing as the lady had done. The Schubert dances. As far as was known, he had never seen a piano except for the one in the Waisenhaus, let alone played before. At the sound, his parents and their friends, the Ostersetzers and the much-impressed children, crowded round and hemmed him at the key-board. Could he play the sonatina too? He nodded. The pianist said that the boy was even imitating special flourishes of hers, a pause, a *rallentando*.

'*Le pauvre petit joue à merveille*,' said Jacques Chauzal, quoting what Count Zinzendorf had written when he had heard Mozart play at about the same age.

Rudolf asked, 'Why didn't you tell us ?'

To which Jules gave the adult reply, 'There's nothing you need feel bad about.'

Discovery of his talent unblocked his silence, melted the sullenness. A spell had been lifted. Nightmares ceased. He alone seemed to take it all in his stride.

In the course of another consultation, Professor Warschawsky explained how correct his earlier diagnosis had been.

'It had only to be revealed that music is his primary means of expression, and speech secondary.'

The professor then launched into the psychological difficulties that might arise. Fortunately, he had written papers about such special cases, he had recommendations to make. The point was that Jules would sense whatever was in his own best interest.

'What you have on your hands, Frau Baronin, is nothing less than a *wunderkind*. The man to give you advice obviously is Benies-Granadia, I will put you in touch.'

The room designated for Jules and his music was at the top of the house, leading off the famous corridor, up a flight of steep steps. In fact the base of the tower at the end of the house, this room had windows on three sides, and was always light and cold. A Bösendorfer piano was delivered, but it proved to be too bulky to be carried up to that room. Nowhere else would do, Rudolf said, since metronomes and migraines were about to take over. In the end a window frame had to be removed, and some scaffolding and a pulley erected on the roof in order to haul the case up. A sound-proof door was fitted, as well as a device to close it automatically with the hiss and groan of compressed air. 'I can't get him to do more than exercise his fingers,' Guffy said. 'In days gone by at least the child was stretching his legs.'

'Where does he get it from?' Rudolf asked. 'Nobody on either side of the family has had music in them.'

Benies-Granadia, himself a pupil of Leschetitzky, was about to retire from the Hochschule für Musik und Darstellende Kunst. Well preserved, he had the clear and contented looks of someone whose life has been all that he might have hoped. Theatrically so. White hair curled down over his collar. He continued to dress in braided velvets and floppy ties, as in his youth. From his sleeve he used to pull out a handkerchief heavily scented with eau-de-cologne, waving it in the air rather than blowing his nose into it. He had been friends with Massenet and Puccini, Schnabel and Cortot, and his stories about them had a humour all his own. On first meeting Jules, he had taken him for a walk in the park. The two had sat for a while on the iron bench which ringed the huge copper beech. When Jules mentioned that the lake had just been stocked with fish, they both crouched down at the edge of the water, to catch sight of reds and yellows fleeting in the shallows beneath the water-lilies. Benies-Granadia rose with mud on the knees of his trousers.

'What happens is a matter of trust, and for that, I must have a happy child.'

In Benies-Granadia's room overlooking the Danube Canal, Jules played, while behind his back Henriette and Rudi sat on a sofa whose upholstery was coming apart. An elderly maid shuffled in and out with glasses of Russian tea.

Opening wide his own hands, Benies-Granadia spread Jules's short little fingers against them, by way of comparing reach and span.

'A day will come when suddenly you'll realise that the notes seem to have shrunk.'

Once a fortnight, Jules was to be brought to him for supervision. Another teacher, Olga Lesnikova, would do the daily work of teaching technique, sight-reading, musicianship. Every year, Benies-Granadia continued, he was confronted by a prodigy or two of this kind. The potential was all or nothing. Some dried up, took a wrong turn, vanished from sight. There were tragic examples of children whose gifts were too great, or whose character could not support their gift. The main thing was never to let the child become self-conscious as a prodigy. And where did it come from ? Everyone had heard of Baron Ellingen. A self-made man, prodigious too. What this boy had in him was much the same. The Jewish soul, he called it.

·Fifteen·

The annual migration from Pernsdorf to Sagodvar was prepared long in advance. Cases and trunks piled up, to be sent ahead for loading: rooms were closed. On the morning of departure, Henriette and Rudolf drove to the station with hours in hand, to check this mass of luggage. Private trains were assembled in reserved sidings but had to leave as punctually as the public service. In due course Przeweck would bring by car anything that had been forgotten. Too much dust was thrown up on the unpaved roads of western Hungary for them to be travelled in comfort.

At Sopron, on the frontier, the train halted. Small gifts were passed to the officials in charge of formalities, and tips for porters, clerks, runners. Far out in the countryside, at level crossings without traffic, uniformed railwaymen were posted under the sun, like sentries along the one-track branch-line. In the afternoon Sagodvar was reached. There on the platform waited the station-master and two local gendarmes, and Egyedy, a slight figure in a suit for the occasion, rather than wear his usual breeches and gaiters. The station-master's daughter held a bouquet. Before the white picket fence of the little halt were horse-drawn carriages. The coachmen kissed the hands of Henriette and Rudolf.

An arch had been erected to mark the entrance to the village, and there the mayor welcomed Henriette with a short speech. She spoke enough Hungarian to be able to reply, much to the admiration of friends and guests and servants in the carriages, those who came every year, Louise von Arnheim, the Revertellas, Jacques Chauzal, Guffy, Amelie, Olga Lesnikova, Burschen Franz, the chef. (Every year too, Rudi packed a teach-yourself-Hungarian book, with the thought

74

that one day he would surprise the mayor.) Villagers gathered to watch. Along the single street, a score of houses faced one another – one-storey, whitewashed, with blues and ochres on woodwork and shutters. Thatched roofs, storks' nests on the chimney-tops, doorways tall and wide enough for a hay-cart to pull into the farmyard behind. Ducks and geese underfoot. The school-house alone was out of keeping, in brick, with ugly blank windows in whose panes flashed the declining sun. On purchasing Sagodvar, Gustav had insisted on building this school and paying for the teacher. In the extension to the rear was the telephone switchboard, still a novelty, though installed before the war. As often as not, it was a pupil from the school who arrived at the house to deliver telegrams, blue-grey forms on which were requests from Margulies or notification of plans confirmed or cancelled, all in smudged indelible ink, the hand-writing spiky, the foreign names mis-spelled to the point of being indecipherable.

Beyond the village an avenue of limes led to the house. On either side of the drive lay the white-fenced paddocks of what had been the stud. Groves of acacias were light green, feathery under a breeze. The house was in sand-coloured stone, its blocks rectangular in cut. French windows opened on to flagged terraces along the entire length of the front and the back. However still and stuffy the summer, these ground-floor rooms remained cool. Little had been changed in them since Baron Gustav's time : silk curtains faded by sunlight, rosewood and pearwood furniture, pictures by von Blaas of Kismet and Kikeriki, Bludan and Ilona, and half a dozen other winners of races on courses as close as Budapest and Sopron, as far away as Hamburg and Longchamps. Nothing could prevent the sound of the grand piano filtering through these interconnected rooms. (Which is harder, Rudolf asked, his scales or Olga's accent? If a pepper-grinder could talk, it would be in her voice.)

The central stone staircase was finished with a brass hand-rail. On the walls above were hung the antlers of stags and roe-deer, mounted on wooden shields, inscribed with the initials of previous owners of Sagodvar. Also stuffed capercailzies and a bustard shot on the *puszta*, its wings spread in a six foot span. Parquet flooring covered the upper floor, scenting the house with summer-warmed polish. As at Pernsdorf, Henriette and Rudolf had different rooms. In Jules's bedroom was an upright piano.

At the back of the house a path led through acacias to a clearing in which stood a circle of weathered stones of varying shapes and sizes. A century of dogs, named and dated, had been buried in a cemetery of their own, Charlie, Arpad, Boy, Rustum, Kisebb, retrievers and labradors for the shoot. This path then came out at the brick frontage of the former stud. For the sake of appearances, the empty stalls had been laid with straw. Gustav's winners were recorded in his own colours: gold lettering on a Prussian blue board. The remaining work-horses for the carriages and the estate were looked after by two grooms, both pensioned. They slept on hay in the loft, and washed from hooped buckets filled at the hand-operated pump.

Egyedy, his wife Piri and his daughter Margit, lived in the stud-manager's house alongside the loose-boxes. In this headquarters, meals were served sometimes to the estate workers at a single long table; medicines were dispensed to men and animals; papers and account-books, inventories, pairs of worn-out boots and gaiters, hats and dog-baskets, were amassed in controlled chaos. Plans of Sagodvar hung from wooden rollers, mapping in detail the fields out to the next villages of Zalaszentistvan and Maroshely. Also a board for keys to granaries of maize and wheat, to apple stores, to piggeries; ancient keys of large size and weight to doors which might or might not still be functioning. A locked room contained cabinets full of shot-guns, a padlocked chain looped as a further precaution through the trigger-guards.

Like her husband, Piri Egyedy appeared to be everywhere at once; a stocky woman, with cropped hair in which were the slightest streaks of henna. From the early hours she ordered women in headscarves from the village to push eiderdowns out to air on bedroom sills, to hump wicker laundry-baskets to the washerwomen, to polish the brass stair-rail and the endless glass panes of the ground-floor rooms. Afterwards she might take Jules and her daughter Margit to the gardens to cut dahlias and chrysanthemums, or to fetch jams and pickles from the larders. With her he went to the village where there were boys his own age, with whom he drank raspberry juice and watched the gypsies and listened to their music.

Of all the pleasures and possibilities at Sagodvar, the miniature train was his favourite. The small-gauge track covered the entire estate. Gustav had ordered it originally from the Gross-Jedlersdorf works, complete with engine-shed and rolling-stock. The scaled-down waggons had sides which could be lowered to load beet, sunflowers, potatoes, maize or *kukurutz* – the system had paid for itself many times over, it was calculated, in the saving of labour and transport costs. In the shed worked the estate mechanic, Pista, trained at Concordia, and it was he who chose when to fit into the waggons the varnished wooden benches for passengers. During practice runs before the opening shoot, Jules and Margit were allowed to stand on the engine's footplate, helping to load wood to raise steam. Even without a load and on level ground, the engine could hardly catch up a cantering horse.

When the dawn was still blue-grey and silent, Rudolf sometimes took Jules out riding, with Egyedy and the old grooms. Hoof-beats drummed on hardened earth. At Sagodvar, Rudolf liked to read the books in vogue, Thomas Mann and Rilke, Barbusse, Capek, Ortega, but he might also put on white flannels, wind a tie round his waist instead of a belt, and teach Jules how to play tennis on a court which stained the balls to a peppermint green. A week or two of this life, and his skin was less sallow, though he never became sun-burnt.

On their sight-seeing expeditions Rudi and Jacques Chauzal also took Jules, to Komarom, Esztergom, Kapuvar. What is baroque, they asked him, and rococo? (Their answers: being serious in stone, and being frivolous in stone.) House parties were exchanged with Sandor and Marie von Pechy at Felsöjattö. Their son Geza was more or less Jules's age, and had a gun made for him by the carpenter there, stained a realistic colour, with a real leather strap. More telegrams were carried up from the village, more guests arrived from abroad, in preparation for the shooting.

On the opening day, out the train pulled with loaders, keepers, gun-cases, boxes of cartridges, dogs, in the direction of Zalaszentistvan, skirting beetroot fields and powdery waist-high maize which crackled. Everywhere partridges scattered in dense coveys towards the level horizon, only to settle again. The train unloaded, the line of guns formed and walked up the fields. At such moments, Ferdy Revertella was disappointed with himself if he had fewer than ninety kills for every hundred cartridges fired. In the midday heat, the train returned with Henriette and the other women, bringing ice and drinks in thermoses. Canvas tenting was erected, and for a while the men lay in its shade like soldiers in a lull, mopping their faces. And seeing Rudi, in English tweeds in spite of the heat, and with a grey felt hat whose brim he pulled down particularly low, Henriette thought: my husband, on my land. At the close of the day, the train drew them home, to find on the lawn a thousand partridges or more, laid out in easily counted squares, ten by ten, a *tableau* under the immense skies of the flame-shot dusk.

·Sixteen·

'I am going to Paris,' Rudolf said.

'Oh, when?'

'Tomorrow.'

'But I can't be ready by then.'

For a moment, Henriette hardly realised that she was not invited. A sale at the Hotel Drouot. How long he would be away depended on what he could buy. In over ten years of marriage, and even during the war, he had never abandoned her outright like that, leaving her in the lurch without warning. And why now? What was he thinking of? In the on-rush of anger, she had fantasies of retaliation and revenge. She would write the True Confessions of an Exploited Woman, filling page after page with accusations and griefs. I own everything, I pay for everything, I do the work, they do the enjoying: she was shaking with self-pity and temper. *How they all use me, and how dare they*? The man had been nervous, he had clearly postponed telling her his plans. On these terms family life was worthless. One had one's father, one's husband, one's son, but each male in turn brought loss, disappointment, frustration. The sense of betrayal hurt, was physically constricting in the chest.

In the fortress of her room once more, she rang for Amelie, and was helped into bed.

Rudolf knocked, then like a doctor stood over her.

'In an hour we are supposed to be in town dining with the Thiebergers.'

'Pretend it's Paris, go by yourself.'

'They'll think it strange.'

'No stranger than when it is learnt that you've gone to Paris without me.'

79

'Why punish the good and kind Thiebergers instead of wicked me?'

In the ritual of these scenes, he was supposed to surrender at this point, to collapse on the edge of the bed, to groan and accuse himself of lack of attention, to hold her hands and protest his love. And instead he left her to it, without apologies. In disbelief, she listened to the sounds of his bath running, to him changing and leaving with Przeweck, the chauffeur whom she paid.

Another meal in her room, another sleepless night. The little Ellingen girl – *did you ever see such a fright*? – herself an orphan, looked after by nobody and nothing except possessions and memories. After the dinner party, perhaps he had returned to his own flat. Only in the morning she heard him instructing Burschen Franz across the landing about clothes to pack. The light in the room was bruising. In the mirror she saw her eyes like open holes in a skull, and cried once more. Standing against the window, she rested her forehead on its cold glass. The green of early summer brightened the park with its protective trees, and the lake silver-speckled with water-lilies. She watched Margulies arriving. He would park out of sight, make his way to the office through the side door. And then Louise too, in a coat with an upturned collar which suited her *soubrette* looks, the slightly show-off way she walked. Before entering the house, she removed a beret, ran a hand over the permanent waves in her fair hair. Thick lipstick designed a bow on her mouth. Out of the generosity of her heart, Louise was more and more in charge of household arrangements, a voluntary social secretary to take private correspondence off Fräulein Lindner's hands, a companion for lunch.

'The Thiebergers were sorry about your absence. You'd felt unwell all of a sudden, I told them.'

'I am coming to see you off.'

'On the way you'll have to crouch in the car to avoid being spotted by everyone who's heard my white lie and is sending you flowers.'

Jacques Chauzal was already at the station, and with him

another Frenchman, Thierry de Fraysinnet, a young man who raised his hat to reveal a parting through the very middle of his hair. Alone on the platform when the Paris express pulled out, she had a sight of the three of them leaning out of a *wagon-lits* window and waving.

'I can't imagine what he sees in them. If he wants to be invited to embassies, he hardly needs Monsieur Chauzal,' Henriette said to Louise.

'If you don't know why, I cannot possibly be the one to tell you.'

They were in the library. Coffee had not yet been cleared away. A parcel of books was waiting to be unwrapped; on his return Rudi would arrange them in the appropriate sections.

'Know what?'

Someone must once have told Louise how much prettier she looked when her face was set in a smile.

'Please don't force me, it's only your best interests I have at heart.'

'You are speaking of Jacques Chauzal?'

Louise hesitated purposefully. 'He's a pansy.'

'A pansy,' Henriette repeated.

'Dearest, I had to tell you, just as we had to warn you before when Prince Solkovsky wanted his money out of Concordia. It harms you to be sheltered to the point of deception. That's what loyalty means, to serve you and protect you. Eduard is always saying how we owe you everything. They are all homosexuals. It's *the* homosexual circle of Vienna.'

'What do they do ?'

'At your age, you can't ask. But what do you imagine happens in the apartment in the Michaelerplatz ?'

A homosexual, then. Also the father of her child, even then polishing a piece for Benies-Granadia. This was a moral landscape in which she would have to be guided by Louise, who had the information. It was a matter of helplessness to be so lacking in worldly knowledge. Louise was comforting her.

'You're terribly shocked, I am afraid, but surely it can't be quite unexpected? I don't mean to pry, but you do have separate rooms, I wonder if he visits you.'

Together they climbed the wide curve of the staircase under the glass dome, and shut themselves in Rudolf's room. Little but clothes. Unlike her, he did not memorialise the past with photographs, trinkets, keep-sakes. Some fine vases, the statuette in bronze of a lion, an Islamic tile. In a drawer, a bundle of letters was held by an elastic band: 'Beloved boy', they began, from his mother, with dreary recitals of daily events of no significance. An autobiography, the fly-leaf inscribed by the author, Paula Wengeroff, a woman of whom Henriette had never heard, apparently a social worker and reformer. Books by Martin Buber, Max Weber, Sombart; also essays and pamphlets to feed his obsession with anti-semitism. A saucer of foreign coins, his evening watch, cuff-links.

The Michaelerplatz, then, would be a den of vice. A long time had passed since she had set foot there. And what excuses had he given when first he had begun to spend nights there in the war ?

'We must see it for ourselves.'

'The concierge will tell him we've been there, we can't break in.'

Outwardly they were two fashionable ladies strolling in the afternoon when Przeweck dropped them at the Hofburg. The dark green outer door to the Michaelerplatz building was closed: the door-knob and a row of bells had been brightly buffed.

The concierge recognised Henriette, saying 'The Herr Baron is abroad.'

'I am preparing a surprise for him, I don't want him to know we've been here.'

Frau Kohak unlocked the appartment for them, gratefully accepted the note which Henriette pulled out of her handbag.

Facing her was the wall on which hung the Moritz von Schwind which she had once rejected. Double-doors separated the front sitting-room from a bedroom. Curtains and upholstery had a comfortable bachelor's style. There was a third room, and as though expecting to catch Rudi red-handed, Henriette and Louise hurried through into it, to find assorted porcelain, a horse with a glaze the colour of marmalade, a

Buddha, canvasses and framed drawings in stacks on the floor.

Sitting at his desk, Henriette opened the drawers. Account books with marbled cardboard covers. Schwarzenberg and Lobkowitz, Czernin and Liechtenstein, the names of those among whom he bought and sold were recorded in his meticulous hand. This was how he was able to be so aloof about Concordia and her fortune; he owed her nothing, the man was a dealer through and through.

'Look!' Louise was holding two photographs, enlarged and mounted on stiff grey board. Jacques Chauzal, undoubtedly, in fancy dress as Mozart, complete with peruke tied back by a black bow. Across one of the photographs were the words *Hommages à l'archévêque de Salzbourg de la part de Wolfgang-Amadeus*. Otherwise only catalogues, books about art, inventories of collections.

So intent were they as they stripped off the bed-clothes that they failed to realise for a moment that someone else had entered the room. The cleaning-woman was staring at them. Excuses were made for the untidiness. In return for more money, Henriette extracted a promise that the woman would say nothing to Rudi.

'Come to Wasserburg and stay with us,' Louise said. 'I can't possibly leave you now, I should never have told you in the first place.'

'You were quite right, I am glad you did, I shall have to consider what to do next. Perhaps I'll write to my mother-in-law, or go out there and ask her advice.'

A homosexual. A good father all the same. It came to her that those marble-papered account books and aristocratic names were a cause for respect. Also some sort of recollection surfaced of a fancy-dress party in the middle of the protracted months when Gustav lay on his death-bed and she could not have thought of attending it. Photographs of Jacques Chauzal as Mozart were hardly incriminating in themselves, could have the most innocent explanation. Rudi was a reliable husband too in his way, distinguished, someone for whom keeping up appearances mattered very much. He would be unwilling to let her or himself down. At least he had not gone off with another woman, and that was a relief. Letters arrived from Paris regularly, to describe amusingly a series of dinners, plays, restaurants, the house where he had been received by the young Marquis de Fraysinnet whom she would remember from the station on account of his vulgar parting. André Gide, no less, had been hospitality itself. Briand, the foreign minister, had been in fine form at a luncheon, though utterly irrational on the subject of the old Austro-Hungarian empire, and he had been obliged to put the fellow right, which had made a great commotion.

At Wasserburg, the chestnuts were in bloom, incandescent white, with here and there an unnatural pink. To the west of Vienna, in an enclosed valley of its own, the house had been a hunting-lodge, or perhaps a folly. A narrow stream had been dammed into a miniature moat. A scaled-down classical pediment was supported on Doric columns. Downstairs, the plasterwork ceilings were elaborate. Restoration of the place had meant almost as much to the elder von Arnheim as his work at Concordia. In old age he had lost his eye-sight, and now hardly left his room, though he did come down to greet Henriette, feeling his way along a rope set up for him on movable wooden struts by his nurse.

The windows of Henriette's room opened wide over fields where deer were supposed to wander. In the evening, mist lifted off the water in the moat, thick enough sometimes to linger until well after the sun had risen on it the following morning.

'You'll rest here,' Louise said. 'We'll have all the time in the world to ourselves, my Eduard is away all day at the factory.'

In Henriette's room the two women took to whispering, as though afraid of being overheard by the old man bumping into his furniture on the other side of the wall.

'We've got the house to ourselves. You can trust me. With so much confusion in it, your poor head must be in danger of bursting. There's never been anybody to love you properly. Let me comfort you, I shan't let you down.'

84

·Seventeen·

Paris had agreed with Rudi, he had never felt better in his life. No other city was so civilised. André Gide had been lecturing on Dostoevsky. Jacques Chauzal would not be returning to Vienna, having been promoted to an office in the Ministère de la Marine, with curious embossed leather on the walls, the like of which he had never seen elsewhere. Thierry de Fraysinnet was proposing to tour the temples of Indo-China.

Nor was he empty-handed. Rudi held out a box. In it was a pair of candlesticks. Figures of two noble savages from the New World stood on column bases of agate and ormulu. Both were lacquered a shiny black, naked to the waist, the man holding a gilded bow and arrows, the woman with a gilded parrot in the crook of her arm. Above their feathered head-dresses were sockets for candles. Originally in Malmaison, these figures of savages were a reference to the Louisiana Purchase, and Rudi explained how lucky he had been to acquire them when the Musée Carnavalet was also on the war-path.

'Kahnweiler thinks this is the finest modelling of the period he's ever had.'

It was midday, but he fetched tapering candles and placed the pieces on the mantelpiece, and lit them for effect.

'You don't like my additions, I know, but these are different. The couple must never be separated. Promise me that whatever happens you'll never part with them.'

The code was transparent. He must have been already to the Michaelerplatz and discovered how she and Louise had been spying there. Had he discovered anything else? The candlesticks must have cost thousands of francs. Better for once to remain silent, to press her hands against those cheeks without blood in them, to stroke his delicate eyelids and eye-lashes, and accept the spoils of easy victory. Another Jacques Chauzal or a young marquis might appear in due course but that was for another day, and at least this husband had done his penance at the Wailing Wall and would not leave her for another woman.

·Eighteen·

The Revertellas had been allowed to retain possession of their house in Venice only because they took out Italian national-ity. Correspondingly, everything they had owned in Austria was sequestrated. Ferdy's Concordia shares were held in a blocked account. To break the legal dead-lock, Henriette consented to buy out this holding on the same terms as for Prince Solkovsky. Ferdy Revertella was thereby provided with money to buy back from the authorities his own house in Vienna, which he promptly sold. The Revertellas had returned to the country of their origins. All the same, Ferdy was liable to start sentences with *Diese blöden Italiener* until the march on Rome and Mussolini's arrival in power re-focused his nationalism and he no longer found the Italians foolish.

It was Margulies's advice to amalgamate the Solkovsky and Revertella shares, and place them in the name of Jules. The op-portunity for so straightforward a transfer to the heir might not recur, and Henriette's majority position was not threat-ened. The shares were to be held in Switzerland, to Jules's name, so that as and when the factory returned to profitabil-ity, Baron Gustav's disastrous transfer might be in part reversed.

The moment of closest association with the Revertellas was in the summer of 1926, when this transaction had been com-pleted. As in the Sargent portrait, Mimi Revertella continued to wear skirts reaching to the ground, and her hats had a brim to keep the sun off her skin. Her time was devoted to Marietta and Toni, already teenagers. The children took Jules to the Lido, where the grown-ups might arrive for lunch. Henriette and Rudi so abhorred bathing that neither of them even owned a swimming costume.

'And really,' Rudi told Henriette, 'people who have had so much Ellingen money given to them for no very good reason ought to have more to show for it.'

He was the one to hire a gondola, to explain what to look for in museums and churches, who explored the Zattere and Canareggio, and had heard of an eccentric lady who lived in rooms decorated by Canova and which she could be persuaded to show them. As usual Rudi claimed to have forgotten how to speak Italian but to be able to learn it again by reading a grammar when he had nothing better to do.

'The children aren't like Gustav,' Henriette said. 'They ought to be short and square if they were true Ellingens, but sometimes I believe I catch his expression in their faces.'

'Certainly they are not in the image of leathery Ferdy either.'

'Neither Mimi's looks, nor his brains.'

On a day of gathering heat, they made an expedition to San Francisco del Deserto. They were to picnic. Afterwards the children disappeared along the reedy shore of the island, and Rudi found a monk to lead him through the monastery. In an arbour with a fig-tree in one corner, Mimi reminisced to Henriette about Gustav at Marienbad and Carlsbad; how he had dealt with bores; the way he fastened his lips round the butt of a cigar to indicate that a conversation was at an end. Henriette missed her opportunity. Coward, Rudi teased her afterwards, the truth of the putative brother and sister would now never be decided.

Towards the end of that holiday, they visited Parma. There, in the centre of the city, they passed a show-room in which was displayed a new model Isotta Fraschini, black with red leather upholstery, silver wheels with a mesh of spokes, and a canvas hood. Instead of returning to Vienna to catch the annual re-served train, Rudi proposed, they could drive straight to Sagodvar, together for once they would do something impulsive. To deter him, and in the hope that the salesman would not understand, Henriette spoke in German. They could not pay, they would be car-sick, they had no chauffeur and neither of them could drive, the Revertellas would be shocked.

'Jules's eyes are shining.'

'He's quite spoiled enough.'

He turned to the boy. 'You do want the car ?'

'I want what you want.'

'Here we have a diplomat.'

'Look at the position you've put him in, having to choose between us, over a mere whim.'

Very well, then, they would have the car, and much good would it do them. She sent for her chauffeur, then herself returned by train to Vienna. There was no getting out of it. What had begun more or less as a joke ended in guilt.

Far from being shocked, the Revertellas enjoyed driving in a convoy slowly through Yugoslavia, stopping on the way at Zagreb, the painted churches of Serbia, a small town with a mosque and minaret which had survived from the historic Turkish occupation.

All week Jules asked, 'Why doesn't she come with us ?'

'Your mama finds it hard to enjoy herself. The rich are like that, it's a punishment that comes with their privileges. You can always tell when the rich don't want to spend money for fun, their lips twist down horribly.'

In the back of the Isotta, side by side, they were uncomfortable, as a matter of fact. The canvas hood was too low, and Prezeweck's head blocked much of the view. Not yet run in, the car had to be driven slowly. In order to stick to hard roads, they made the longer journey through Budapest. In addition, the air attaché at the Italian embassy had invited the Revertellas to attend a display of Italian aircraft.

The airfield was at Gödöllö, and they drove out there early from Budapest. Along a fenced-in runway, several hundred spectators watched a demonstration of military aircraft. One new fighter-bomber had been fitted with half a dozen seats for those who wanted to fly a circuit over the airfield; the pilot also indulged in a few minutes of aerobatics. It was arranged that Toni and Marietta should take Jules with them on one of these flights. Whether Jules had loosened his safety straps, or had fixed them incorrectly, or was too small for them, he was dislodged from his seat as the aircraft rolled, and hit his head on the cockpit cover.

Consternation on the faces of Toni and Marietta told Rudi that there had been an accident. Carrying the boy himself to the car, he could not help smearing his clothes, and then the shiny upholstery, with blood from the head-wound.

'No danger from untimely accident, Jules concussed,' ran the telegram despatched to Sagodvar. In unforgiving triumph Henriette hastened to the hospital, with Louise, dispossessing Rudi of further responsibility. The two stayed at the foot of Jules's bed, and overwhelmed him day after day with presents. For a long time he suffered from head-aches. That summer there was no clambering with Pista on the estate-train, no walking with the guns, no playing with Geza von Pechy at Felsöjattö. Blame somehow was attached to the Revertellas, creatures of ill-omen and presage, without whom there would have been none of this chain of incidents outside Henriette's control.

Like the failed toy it was, the Isotta remained laid up in the stables at Sagodvar.

·*Nineteen*·

Princess Irina Solkovsky, to Henriette, 21 February 1927:

Most beloved friend, Your beautiful letter has affected me deeply. Great strength flows from every word you have written. I say to myself that I must be grateful for over forty years of marriage. Quite what someone of such wide culture and so many interests saw in a woman as ordinary as myself I shall never know, but truly Felix was most devoted. I have been fortunate. Also widowhood, with its loneliness, is perhaps better than a life unable to do anything for my poor Felix, as was the case. At the end he was in such agony that it was hard to bear it with him. What God's purpose is in such a trial may be the hardest thing we are ever asked to comprehend, but I try to do so with all my might, praying not to lose faith through failure to understand human mysteries. Friendship with you and your dear family has been a jewel in our crown. Felix never let pass a day without heartfelt gratitude to Gustav, your father of blessed memory. From our dear Louise, I hear nothing but good of you, not that this surprises me in the least, angel of mercy that you are. Do not forget us.

'At Rentzenburg I feel like a bucket of water that has been collected drip by drip through a hole in the roof.'

In spite of this opinion, Rudi was obliged to stay there on several occasions in the aftermath of Prince Solkovsky's death.

'And is it so terrible that she wants Paul to be taken on at Concordia?' Henriette asked.

'All of them want the blessings of your father to be visited on their sons.'

In his early twenties at the time, Paul Solkovsky had been a law student in Prague. The career dissatisfied him. With the death of his father, he had returned to live at Rentzenburg. A crucial ten years separated him in age from Jules. The main entertainments in the house were the removal and subsequent re-assembling of helmets and weapons from suits of armour in the Rittersaal, and accompanying Paul on the cello. Under the family tree and its portraits, Paul and Jules practised the Beethoven cello sonata in A major.

'If ever there's a concert here, we shall all be discovered frozen dead in our seats,' Rudi said.

'I don't know what to do,' Jules told his parents. 'He thinks he's a musician, but he's wrong.'

Any idea of performance was scrapped when Paul Solkovsky suddenly shouted that he had never met anyone so conceited as Jules, and did he believe he knew better than Beethoven when it came to tempo and phrasing?

Princess Irina Solkovsky, to Henriette, not dated, but written at the end of 1927, or possibly early in 1928:

Beloved Henriette, Memories of you and yours are still fragrant in this house of quiet sorrow. Your presence here has been such a comfort when we must suffer the absence of loved ones. Bonds between us can never loosen. Little Jules has sent me an enchanting letter. How right and proper it is to be humbled by that talent, prodigious, truly God-given. I do so pray for him ... [a passage about the meaning of religion to her has been omitted] Like his father, Paul can do what he wants as long as he sets his mind to it. He has been mastering himself, I am proud to say. Soon he plans to be in Vienna, and when he telephones, you will be able to make arrangements. I know how greatly he is looking forward to staying with you while he decides what to do about the offer to join Herr Tucher's office.

·*Twenty*·

The Landerziehungsheim at Matzleinsdorf was a boarding-school. As if that was not uncommon enough in Austria, the headmaster held the view that he was preparing a young elite for its proper role in the future. Should Jules's career demand that he subordinate his studies to music, then Dr Leinsmer would not stand in his way. Quite the contrary. It was acceptable that Jules should be a day-boy by special arrangement, driven over every morning, and home again in the evening.

Disconcertingly, Jules's interest in music retreated. His hours of practising dwindled. Benies-Granadia was too predictable, Lesnikova too dull. He boasted that he might take up conducting, but did not bother to study scores, or even listen to much music on the gramophone.

More aggressive signs of change appeared. In what he supposed was an imitation of his father's wit, he became flip and sarcastic.

'Why is the von Arnheim woman always hanging round your neck?' he asked his mother. 'The sight of her pursed-up mouth puts me off my food. Traces of her lipstick are on the rims of every cup and glass in this house.'

Boys from the Landerziehungsheim used to make illegal expeditions, at weekends especially, to the cinemas in the city centre, and he joined them, refusing to explain what he was doing, nor when he would return. Challenged, he flung at his parents that he was marooned in a place too embarrassing to bring anyone into, and he had no intention of living as they did.

At thirteen, Jules had already grown to within a few inches of his full height. Gustav's descendant, he would never be tall. Nor had he yet filled out across the chest. Like his father, he held himself well and there was never a moment when clothes looked untidy on him. His black hair no longer curled but had flattened, with only a slight and easily manageable waviness close to his temples. He appeared more introspective than he was on account of his inherited pallor.

That Jules would do his bar-mitzvah at the Waisenhaus, along with other boys of his age there, was not in doubt. A family position had to be maintained, *Jude muss man sein aber nicht zum Abattoir*. It was the custom for Henriette to present every boy with a watch. If this child of mine stays at the Landerziehungsheim, Rudi decided, he would become ashamed of himself as a Jew, as well as lazy and lacking in manners.

An authentic boarding-school was the solution, the genuine article in England. Speaking the language, Jules would be able to hold his own, grow up, acquire the proper style of a gentleman. In another generation, Rudi said, a Jew might also be able to combine being rich and happy, but meanwhile these things were better dealt with across the Channel.

Investigation yielded the name of a school specialising in pupils needing sensitive handling, a high proportion of them foreigners. High Hampton was an hour from London, in a manor on the edge of a Buckinghamshire village. The drive up to the house was bordered with rhododendrons, and these were in flower when Henriette and Rudi first inspected the place. The garden had box-hedges, with a sundial at the centre. Beyond rose the goal-posts of the playing-fields.

Receiving them in his study, Mr Kingdom proved to be elderly and stout, in grey flannels and a jacket. Previously he had been a headmaster in India, and talked to them almost exclusively about his admiration for Gandhi. And what about bullying, fagging, the traditions of English schools? Nothing of the kind existed here. In almost every sentence he addressed them as Baron and Baroness. Mrs Kingdom then escorted them round dormitories of four or six beds, the communal baths, the sanatorium, a dining-hall. And how many Jewish boys were there in the school? 'We have no idea, Baron, nobody has bothered to count.' That answer disposed of any last doubts.

For the term starting in September 1930, Jules left home for the first time. Henriette and Rudi took him as far as London, and with them travelled Miss Magoffin. After a life-time at Pernsdorf, she was retiring to live with her sister, leaving what had been her home without a backward glance. A trunk was bought and around it was painted a distinguishing stripe in Gustav's colours of blue and gold; the same outfitter provided the regulation clothes, unfamiliar shorts, football boots.

'And do you call yourself a Kraut, a Hun, a Boche?' the other boys wanted to know. 'You lost the war, how about a taste of the same medicine?'

Jules's closest friend was made immediately. Stavrakis was six months older, but much more mature, a Greek but already cosmopolitan.

'I've heard about you and your family,' he said. 'Welcome to the Kingdom of the Blind.' He habitually referred to the school like that, in the hearing of masters including Mr Kingdom, who tolerated it.

Stavrakis was a ring-leader. His other friend, Immington, was a giant of a boy, so fair that he was almost albino. Immington's father was a boat-builder in Barbados. Stavrakis taught Jules and Immington the Greek national anthem, and sometimes they hummed it, lips shut, in the classes.

The school photograph for the summer term of 1931 has survived in Henriette's keeping. In the centre of the group sits Mr Kingdom, in a light linen suit and a panama hat with a black band. He wears imposing spectacles, his chin is self-importantly thrust forward. Mrs Kingdom's garment is native-style, loose and in cotton, with a necklace of heavy beads round her neck. Some of the Indian boys have bothered to put on ties and jackets for the occasion, but the majority appear to have just come off the cricket-pitch. Among the masters, Rex Smail-Turner leans back in his chair, with a know-all expression, implying superiority to the scene, or boredom, or both at once. His hands rest on his knees. In the button-hole of a regimental blazer is a white carnation. The bottoms of his trousers widen over a pair of co-respondent shoes. Undoubtedly a handsome and dressy man. Behind him stand Stavrakis, Immington and Hechter.

Rex Smail-Turner taught French and German, speaking both languages with an English drawl. He was also the master in charge of societies and clubs. Boys were welcomed into his room. As far as possible everyone was to do as they liked, in his view; on school outings, he had been known to allow the boys into a pub for a glass of cider. Calculated mystery enshrouded him. If he had not been a man of independent means, at least he had had expectations. Good connections too, but family, friends, his country, somehow had been disappointing. In the war he had been an officer in the Durham Light Infantry, captured at Cambrai, held prisoner for the duration. That was how he had learnt his German. 'You and your lot were delightful,' he told Jules, 'except when you were trying to gas me like an animal.'

Music was taught by Mrs Stokes, once of the Royal College of Music, and widow of the organist of Worcester Cathedral. As a special concession, Jules could stay with her over a weekend. The cottage was crowded out by two pianos on the ground floor. Mrs Stokes's first report, dated 19 December 1930, reads: 'I am quite certain that one day Jules will do himself justice. Talent like his is such a strain on the character, we must be tolerant and understanding. At present he finds it difficult to settle down here and to adapt himself to our rather different approach. Opposing elements pull him apart, which I can best describe as having a left hand like a martinet, a right hand like a poet. Playing the Mendelssohn *Variations* this term he has been all poet and I don't expect my old Broadwood can ever have had such emotion wrung from its keys! Mendelssohn is his composer for the time being – all that lovely youthfulness!'

At the end of the following summer term she was writing, 'Of course he is going through a difficult patch. All boys do at his age, and we wouldn't attach importance to it, if Jules did not have such promise. Schumann, on to whom I have now weaned him, has been demanding, or to say the same thing differently, he has been responding in a somewhat forced manner. At the risk of riding a hobby-horse, I would judge that on the continent methods have been instilled into him rather to his detriment. But what fun we manage to have, what fun indeed it all is to have someone so challenging at this stage of his development.'

The difficult patch to which Mrs Stokes referred had actually evolved out of a specific incident. Games were not compulsory at High Hampton, and in the previous autumn term Stavrakis had stayed away from the playing-fields in order to teach himself to smoke. At the far end of the school grounds was a copse where he and Immington took to spending the afternoon. Anyone coming from the direction of the school could be seen in plenty of time. Past this hide-out ran a stone wall, on whose other side was the parish church and the nearest houses of the village. Jules was introduced to smoking by his two friends. One Saturday, village boys surprised the smokers, jumping over the wall and trying to snatch the cigarettes. Immington picked up a piece of wood and began hitting out with it, chasing the village boys back into the church-yard. There the fight continued, with all boys taking up positions in order to throw stones at one another. Who threw it was never established, but one stone smashed a pane of stained glass in the church windows.

No incident of this kind had occurred in the school's entire history, Mr Kingdom wrote to the parents of the three boys. He was mortified at a flagrant violation of the philosophy of peace and good-will which the school had been founded to promote. Not only was pacifism the way to tame the brute in every one of us, but out of the simple instinct of self-preservation Jules should have reflected that his hands might be damaged in a brawl. Wherever the faults might lie, the vicar was blaming the boys with the chance of a better education, who ought to be setting an example. After a long examination of his conscience, he had decided to suspend sacking the three boys, on condition that they broke no more rules and that the bill for damages was paid.

Immington's father, the boat-builder in Barbados, replied that he had no intention of paying, and that if his son had done

97

something wrong, then a thorough beating would teach him the right lesson. So Stavrakis's father and Henriette shared the expenses between them.

To bring Jules home without any possible mischief, Henriette and Rudi asked the school to provide an escort. Rex Smail-Turner was free. Accordingly at Christmas the two of them travelled out first-class. At the Westbahnhof, Przeweck met them. In the dusk, a winter wind was blowing. Rex wore a trilby and a camel-hair overcoat, belted at the back. As before, Pernsdorf had its lights fully blazing, and fires burning in the grates.

'The vicar's a fearful drip,' Rex explained to Henriette and Rudi. 'You should be grateful that a few Woodbines will have inoculated them against tobacco. And the church would have been much improved if all the hideous Victorian stained glass had been knocked out.' The whole thing would blow over, he maintained, poor *decent* Harry Kingdom couldn't keep his act up for more than a few weeks.

And would they allow him to arrange a proper English Christmas for them ? Would it offend them if a tree was erected in the hall, and he managed to find a plum-pudding ? On Sunday mornings he took Jules to the skating-rink at the Eislaufverein, delighted at the tinny reverberations coming over the loudspeakers. Waltzes were his favourite tunes. He himself could pick out Noel Coward songs on the piano. Like a conscientious tutor, he accompanied Jules to the cinema, sat with him in a café. Friends of his turned up, and lunched at Pernsdorf. A young banker was in Vienna in connection with the collapse of the Credit-Anstalt. Someone else was supposed to be selling raw cotton. 'A chap I used to know in Yorkshire, a fellow from the army whom I happened to bump into in the Kärntnerstrasse,' were Rex's descriptions of these people. Information about his past filtered through. Apparently he had gone more or less straight into the trenches from Oundle. Unqualified to be anything in particular after the war, Rex felt that he was lucky to have fallen into a quiet berth at High Hampton.

A lot is owed to this man, Rudi and Henriette said to one

another, he was giving up his free time to Jules, he was the life and soul of the place. The house seemed too large without him. Refusing to take money, he allowed them to pay for a pair of hand-made shoes he had ordered, and some shirts, and *lederhosen*. Thanks to Rex, school holidays became a pleasure for them.

When Rex became a regular member of the household, as from 1932, he was thirty-nine, six years younger than Rudi, two years younger than Henriette. From Burschen Franz, he took over the serving of drinks before meals, experimenting with cocktails, introducing shiny-coloured liqueurs in odd-shaped bottles. A dedicated gardener, he liked to change into old clothes and replant flowers and shrubs, to take cuttings, and busy himself in the green-house. Every morning, home-grown carnations were placed on the hall table so that he and Rudi could select a button-hole. Rex had the use of the car. The chauffeur's name was absolutely unpronounceable, he said, in future the man would be known as Prizzy-Wizzy. And yes, he agreed to stay on a permanent basis once Jules had passed his School Certificate examination and had nothing more to gain from an English school. The salary would be twice what he had been earning at High Hampton.

·*Twenty One*·

Jules to Stavrakis, 31 January 1933:

You're in luck, there's nothing to do except to write you this letter. Brightest Auchterwhateveritis has about twelve and a half people, and two of them are Guffy and her sister. I am bringing comfort to the two crones. 'We like to keep to ourselves' is their motto, but quite who else they'd keep to is a mystery. It never stops pelting either, I feel myself turning into the slimy green damp stone so popular up here. And how about this? Baron Gustav slipped Guffy some sovereigns when she had to be bundled home on the eve of the war, and she has them still, every one, in a little sock which looks suspiciously baronial too.

Harry K. pressed me to give a recital, and in view of the numerous book-tokens I've accepted from him, I could hardly refuse. Down to the sago and the custard-cream, the place is as you knew it in the days of our youth. Immington is in London, we had a night out, ending in very odd spot. All rather hectic. It's difficult to slip the lead, the parents watch like hawks.

Jules to Stravrakis, 2 March 1934:

The American girl is the one I want to attack and ravish. Everything about her bounces and wiggles. Do they do it on purpose, or does it just happen? She's the girl from the Julliard, she is most extremely serious about being pianistic, and I give her instruction on fingering. I wish you'd come back. Wanda rings up every five minutes. Nettie sobs in the Keller. They miss your brutality. A party of us are going to Kitzbühel. Inescapably Rex has to come. In the middle of the crisis, he distinguished himself. Public transport suspended, streets closed off by the police, half the proletariat homeless, and he comes in with the news 'They've been popping off their guns.' At his invitation, a boy called Oliver Parsons has moved into one of the top-floor bedrooms, a Hamptonian before our day. He's supposed to come skiing too.

Jules to Stavrakis, 27 June 1934 :

You know the mammoth that's been lately dug up in Siberia, a few million years old? It's me, it's me. Yours truly is deep under the perma-frost, which has the advantage that the hard edge of daily life cannot dig down there. Nothing to do with Meriel. At dinner a couple of days ago she announced to everybody that the house was dreamy. And what was so dream-like? Only my success, I can assure you. She thinks I have not noticed her duets with Baby-face Reissner.

The reality is that I am about to chuck the whole thing over and become a tycoon, a tyrant, an utter pirate on the approved family model. Have you seen a steel furnace? The power, the beast's roar at its meal, the absolute devouring hunger of it. A specialist process to do with cables is being evolved. The glories of this sort of engineering became apparent to me as I watched, regretting bitterly that nobody has ever bothered to steer me away from the piano towards the drawing-board, from what is artificial towards what is real. It's a mutual admiration society, and I've had enough. It's not too late for the Technische Hochschule. Rex is made to trot along. My Mama, you will be fascinated to learn, thinks he can be a benefit to the factory, and proposals are afoot to offer him a place on the board. The poor man has even less technical knowledge than I have, but at least I can go through the motions, ask the right questions. We ooh and ah like prize idiots. I am going to take myself in hand. My Mama as usual at this time of year, is retiring to Wasserburg with Louise von Arnheim. Meanwhile my father and Rex are off on another Grand Tour. Starting in the Salzkammergut. You should see the fuss about the right kind of *lederhosen* and white stockings, where the car is to pick them up, who they are to stay with, and whether it is all right to go on into Germany.

Jules to Stavrakis, 27 September 1934 :

I shall never be able to thank you enough. I can't get the landscape out of my system. The glory that was Greece, eternal verities and all that. There is something too magnificently sinister for words about the Mycenae tombs. Agammemnon or the man from the taverna might equally well emerge into the white-hot light of day dripping with blood and vengeance. I have a vision of the beach at Glyphada. You and your cousins. Can we ever go back to Aegina, or is it a case of excommunication ? In the end one seems to find the side of the pit, and far from having to scramble, can lightly vault out. The passivity of normal life is so alarming. The metronome ignores the tune, the clock ticks on regardless. Everybody is somewhere else (that might be the local speciality, mind you). What I want is to switch on the wireless and hear the latest news about myself. In actual fact I have to hurry to the dentist. Chloroform will not be necessary, I have only to recline in the chair and think of Grecian summer.

•*Twenty Two*•

Packets of mail were forwarded from Pernsdorf to Sagodvar in thick envelopes with Henriette's name specially printed on them. In the late autumn of 1934 one such packet contained a letter from Nuremberg, 'Capital of the Movement' according to the post-mark. Vermilion stamps bore the head of Hitler. In the following year, it emerged, the orphanage there would be celebrating its centenary. Berlin alone could boast of a Jewish orphanage that was an earlier foundation. In honour of her father, Henriette had been invited to make a speech.

'Liebermann has died,' Rudi said, 'Goldschmidt has emigrated to Brazil, and the Friedländer-Fulds to New York, we have no friends over there any longer. If Hitler murders his own people like Roehm, what is he intending to do to his declared enemies?'

'We fought them once,' Rex answered, 'I expect we'll have to fight them again. We ought to go and have a look at the lie of the land.'

'We aren't a military mission.'

'Think what Gustav would have said.'

Henriette replied to the governors of the Nuremburg orphanage that she was proud to accept.

The season's shooting was over, and they lingered on with the house to themselves. Every day the train crawled across the fields with the harvesters. Once the crops were in, a series of feasts were served to the men. From Egyedy's quarters, drunken laughter and music echoed across to the big house until late into the night.

In that interlude in their lives, Rudi rode every morning. The groom brought his horse round to the terrace where he mounted. A gelding, powerfully built, capable of going all day long, if necessary. Sometimes Rudi took sandwiches and a flask and did not return for lunch. The place has never looked so beautiful, he said, the land seems to stretch for ever, the colours magical, we shall miss it when we have to leave.

Rex had a talent for filling in time, at his ease doing crosswords, flipping through back-copies of the *Tatler* long since abandoned by Guffy. He taught Henriette backgammon, bezique and cribbage, complicated patiences. To amuse himself, he sketched plans for redesigning the garden around the single immense magnolia which was its principal feature. Henny, he started using the nickname, the Hen, my Hen.

'Funny to think that Rudi and I used to be on opposite sides,' he said. 'We might have shot at each other. This time round, we're all going to be on the same side.'

Before dinner, he and Rudi used to walk together through the acacias. On the evening when Henriette went out to look for them, the sun seemed to have bled over the sky as it set. From a distance she observed them where they stood motionless, engrossed in their conversation, at last startled at the sight of her.

'Whatever are you discussing so deeply?'

Not receiving an answer, she took them both by the arm and returned to the house with her two men, one on either side. In the silence and perfection of the moment, she first realised that she was in love with Rex. That was our true beginning, she used to say in years to come, we were linked together in understanding and communion, by ourselves in those beautiful woods while the sun was setting beyond us at what seemed to be the edge of the world. A *ménage à trois* : they used the phrase openly about themselves. If the world were to think ill of it, so much the worse for the world.

Another letter arrived from Nuremberg in the spring of 1935. By order of the Party, the centenary celebrations had been cancelled, the date clashed with the Parteitag, and that was inappropriate. But that order was reversed too, when it turned out that the Party was insisting on the ceremony for the sake of normality. The governors were now pleading with Henriette to attend.

'Somebody is sure to report on the speech,' Rex said, 'but there's little or nothing they can do about it. It's harmless.'

'Pick the wrong words and the orphanage will be closed down.'

A sense of fatality supervened. The journey was in the lap of the gods. On the eve of crossing the frontier, they were in a hotel surrounded by Germans. The swastika reminded Rudi of a tarantula ; the syllables of Hitler's name drummed in the head like a migraine. It was impossible to proceed but to turn back meant abandoning the orphanage, surrendering to cowardice. At the German border, in fact, the officials saluted courteously in the old style. Somehow dragon's teeth should have been visible but here were the mountains of Bavaria, then Franconian villages.

The Nuremberg orphanage was in Wilhelmine Gothic, soot-blackened, severe. In front, tall iron railings enclosed a gravelled yard, to the rear was the worn grass of a playground. The surroundings were much as Gustav must once have known them, except for the banners flying on the roof-tops for the Parteitag, the flags draping whole facades in red, white and black stripes.

The director who received them was young, thin, with an Adam's apple that bobbed up and down as he spoke. The speech would be tomorrow, he said, final authorisation had still been withheld but it would be granted. The room in which Henriette and Rudi were to sleep seemed to have been squashed on to a staircase like a cupboard. The walls were a penitential brown, the shutters closed. Rex and the chauffeur were in staff-rooms at the far end of the building.

Next morning they walked the short distance to the centre of the town. One military convoy after another clogged the narrow medieval streets. In the lorries soldiers were singing. Passers-by waved and shouted back as in a carnival. In the past, Rudi and Henriette had known the Deutscher Hof, the hotel on the main square. Pushing through they found it cordoned off but while they were standing there hesitating, someone recognised them : Toni Revertella.

Politely Toni kissed Henriette's hand. He was in the

process of finalising arrangements for the Italian delegation. If they cared to wait, he could pull strings for them, obtain tickets to the *Ehrenloge*, have them invited to the Führer's reception for distinguished foreigners. With him, they could certainly enter the Deutscher Hof.

'This is something not to be missed,' Rex said, 'I'll be fine, I'll make my own way.'

As it happened, then, Rex was at the opening march-past of the Parteitag, rather than listening to Henriette as she quoted her father on the virtues of endurance and thrift.

And what was it like? they asked. Noisy, sweaty, too many military bands, all that shouting and yelling. In the stands where he was, he said, if only he had had his army rifle, he could have had a pot-shot at Hitler.

'And I spent my day being shown the orphanage records,' Rudi said. 'I found that Gustav used to subscribe large sums but he stopped doing so as soon as the war was declared. Isn't that curious?'

·Twenty Three·

Jules lived at home, in the rooms which had always been his at the top of the house. Practising, he could not be heard in the tower with windows on three sides. The convention was that he could invite whom he liked to meals or to stay, on condition that he cleared it first with Henriette. The other part of the house colonised by Jules was the billiard room. The cloth on the table was so heavy that two people were required to roll it up. A gramophone was installed, and also two flat sofas or day-beds covered in velour. Impromptu parties might last all night. Rex was supposed to supervise but a blind eye was turned to whatever did or did not happen. Photographs exist of Jules in a white tie, a young man about town ; and on the steps of the house, in a kind of artist's jacket, a young Werther secretly satisfied with his sorrow.

My father obliged me to be trained, Henriette told him, and you too will learn the business. You draw Concordia dividends, you must work for them, be responsible.

After his eighteenth birthday, Jules did in fact attend board-meetings. He proposed to bring younger men in. Margulies and von Arnheim, Leviseur, even Burschen Franz, they ought to have been pensioned off long ago with the rest of the nineteenth century. At such comment, Henriette had a way of raising her eye-brows to look both pleased and critical ; it was right that he should take an interest, wrong that tried and tested arrangements be tampered with.

A paragraph clipped from a society column in one of the papers (without its date but almost certainly during 1936) reads : 'We have heard of an original method of raising funds for charity, and to have an entertaining evening into the bar-gain. The Arkadencafé will be the scene on the next two successive Fridays and Saturdays of a cabaret organised by Alfred Leitenberger. The proceeds go towards the Sanatorium Loew and its fund for research into tuberculosis. Fresh from her success in the revival of *Frühlings Erwachen* is Sophie Paul-Schiff, who with Pauline Weisweiller and Franz Pidoll will put on sketches of their own devising. Highly esteemed in his circle, and heir to the Ellingen industrial fortune, Jules Hechter will accompany them at the piano.'

At the Conservatory, there was an auditorium in which scheduled performances were given by each student in turn, in order to acquire concert training. Every enrolled student was supposed to attend these occasions, to which a certain amount of publicity was attached. No record remains of what Jules chose to play, but in the middle of his piece the swing doors of the auditorium opened and banged to let in a bustling little figure who stood at the back without removing his overcoat or homburg hat, and a companion, a taller man with a round face : Toscanini, in Vienna in that winter of 1936 as guest conductor at the opera, with the violinist Bronislav Hubermann. When Jules reached the end of his piece, the audience looked at the two easily recognisable visitors for their reaction. Toscanini stepped up on to the stage, walked to Jules and with a fatherly hand gave him a series of firm and quickening taps on the cheek. Then in his Milanese Italian he paid a compliment, 'Meno bestia di quel che credevo' – less bad than I might have expected.

·Twenty Four·

A winter journey along the shore of the southern Mediterranean, from Carthage to the great classical sites. Twenty-
three years of marriage deserved to be celebrated
unpredictably. 'And this time,' Rudi said, 'without Rex,
please.'

'Rex has such a good head on his shoulders,' Henriette said.
'And he makes himself useful in a hundred ways. We shall be
bored without him.'

Once a schoolmaster always a schoolmaster. Rex would
understand that these two middle-aged pupils of his might for
once want to play truant, and he and Jules could take care of
themselves at Pernsdorf. Of course Rex did not mind ; on the
contrary, he encouraged them, saying, 'Go gathering rose-
buds. But isn't Carthage supposed to be a great bore ? Tell
you what, why don't I come as far as Naples ?'

On the day of departure, the clouds were a frozen grey, not
much above the tops of the trees. 'When we are back,' Rudi
said, 'something must be done to liven up this park : deer perhaps, red squirrels, even the goats again.'

At Naples the weather continued stormy. 'You're going to
be ill as dogs,' Rex said. 'I'm glad to be staying on dry land.'

For three exhausting days, the Lloyd-Triestino liner buck-
eted and pitched. Thrown off her bunk, a lady in another
cabin broke her hip. Even in the harbour of Tripoli, the sea
had a storm-stirred darkness, in contrast to the primal colours
on shore, the whiteness of the *souk*, and a crisp sky.

They had a letter of introduction from Ferdy Revertella to
the Italian Governor-General, and he received them in what
had been a former Turkish residence. At the entrance, sentries
saluted. In the company of the Governor-General, and

escorted by military cars, they spent two days at oases along the fringe of the desert, where agricultural schemes had been started for peasants from Sicily. A car of their own was provided for the coastal drives to Leptis and Sabrata, for the arch of Marcus Aurelius. At a party, an archaeologist offered for sale a bronze figurine of a child, in his view dating from the second century. Obviously a forgery cast within the last twelve months, Rudi said, but a lucky charm nonetheless, and he paid for it a fraction of the sum asked.

In the direction of Oran, the railway line passed cultivated fields and orchards, usually within sight of the sea. At Algiers, a suite had been reserved in the Georges V hotel, named after its Paris counterpart but decorated with inlaid furniture, old flintlocks, Arab ceramics on the walls. The bedrooms had a deep view over a garden with palm-trees and bougainvillea, down to the sweep of the bay below. A French admiral, discovering that they were friends of Jacques Chauzal, invited them on board his ship. A reception followed at the *préfecture* ; also the inaugural night of a new theatre. As always in a foreign country, Rudi bought a grammar and taught himself what he could, advancing into the difficulties of the *hamzah* and the *alif*. Accosted by beggars and touts, he liked to flourish textbook phrases at them. A guide escorted them through the Kasbah. Together they walked up the mountain to the botanical gardens, and explored the shops along the rue Michelet and the boulevard Sadi Carnot.

The illness began with nothing more than a mosquito bite. Rudi awoke with a swollen neck and a temperature. 'It's nothing,' he said, 'I'm sure I can't have scratched it and anyhow I am never ill.' Under the pressure of the swelling, his neck reddened. Time had already been lost before the doctor was called. He was French, he spoke immediately of blood-poisoning, the urgent need to be in hospital.

'Out of the question,' Rudi said, refusing point-blank to leave his room. What must conditions be in a hospital in Africa? He would engage private nurses, and they could change the poultices and prepare the medicine to bring down his temperature.

The door to Henriette's room stayed open, so that she had him in her view. Meals were sent up to her, European papers delivered. On her own initiative, she despatched the telegram summoning Rex. Receiving no reply, she sent several other telegrams, not only to him but to Jules and the Hechters and Louise, printing in capitals on the post-office forms that Rudi was at death's door. And death, she thought, if that were really to occur in this outlandish place, must have something pre-ordained about it. All from a mosquito bite, which had become infected.

Taking Rudi's hand at one point, she discovered clutched in it the figurine of the child, his new lucky charm. She prised it away, dipped it into disinfectant, angry that even now this husband of hers refused to take himself seriously.

In front of the nurses, Rudi confined himself to German.

'I am so glad that Rex is not here to see me.'

She never told him about the telegrams.

'You do not introduce a man like that into your family, and I should have known.' He winced as he spoke.

Septicaemia, the doctor explained. There had to be an incision, a swab taken, cauterisation in the proper sterile conditions. Half-conscious, Rudi was lifted onto a stretcher and carried downstairs past staring hotel servants and the guests in the blue-and-white tiled hall.

The relief on Rex's arrival brought on hysterical sobbing.

'Jules will be here soon, and Louise too,' he said. 'I've come on ahead, it's not the easiest of journeys.'

For a week, Henriette was to leave her room only once, to descend into the town to buy a black dress and matching hat with a veil.

'The poor chap is too far gone to speak to me,' Rex said.

Somehow, somewhere, the faked figurine of the child was mislaid, most likely stolen. Not so Rudi's signet-ring, which was brought back from the hospital by the doctor, and then and there Henriette gave it to Rex, in commemoration.

·Twenty Five·

What Rudi had wanted, Henriette said, was that his ashes should be scattered in the park. 'I know just where too, we often talked of it. I shall plant oaks on the spot.'

The box had been stored in the attic, a flimsy cardboard box with twine round it, tied to form a loop by which to carry it, exactly as it had been handed over at the crematorium in Algiers.

Twice Henriette postponed doing what had to be done. The June grass was growing in clumps underfoot on the afternoon when they walked past the copper-beech down to the far side of the lake. From there, the house loomed at the top of the slope high above them ; Gustav's fantastic castle and its erratic silhouette.

Inside the cardboard box was the urn, with its screw-top. 'Give it to me,' Rex insisted, 'he was my friend.' 'He was my father,' was the answer, 'and this is the last thing I can do for him.' Then Jules plunged his hand into the urn, and in a wide arc began to spread what was more like flake than ash. When this was finished, Rex removed the urn and its lid and without a word threw them into the lake.

According to place and time and personality, there are things that have to happen as they do, but whose consequences can be neither foreseen nor avoided. In the entrance of the house, Rudi's coats and hats were still hanging ; in the bedroom, the saucer of foreign coins on the dressing-table stood next to his hair-brushes ; a marker showed the page he had reached in the last book he had been reading. Rudi's will bequeathed Jules everything, and he left it untouched.

The lease on the Michaelerplatz apartment had a number of years to run. Pictures and drawings, the china and porcelain accumulated in quantities that spread over the floors, were disposed of to dealers or sent to auction. Choosing to move in, Jules renovated the place. That was the period when he was chasing after a girl by the name of Quappi Verwey, who was Dutch and had hopes of becoming an actress.

In the course of 1937 Rex discovered Chester Warren. An American lawyer, Chester Warren claimed to specialise in protecting those whose interests in Germany were threatened by the Nazi regime. He was a bachelor. For a break, he regularly stayed at the Bristol, and it was in that hotel that a new scheme for Concordia was devised. The key was a transfer of assets into what was nominally foreign ownership but without any actual change in possession. 'That way they can't get you,' Chester Warren explained. 'I do these things the whole time for far-sighted investors.'

Chester Warren was ungainly, his head tilted and his chin stuck out when he spoke. His hair was cropped close to his head, and his three-piece American suits made an effect of buttoning him in.

'Nothing has to be decided or performed,' Rex informed Henriette, 'but there's this man you should listen to.'

When Chester Warren lunched at Pernsdorf, he almost scuppered himself by saying, 'Truly a historic home, and what art treasures! It must be hard to contemplate a life anywhere else.'

'Who is contemplating it?' Henriette asked.

All he meant, Chester Warren said, was that he was a pessimist, that he knew Germany well and believed that accommodations were not possible with Hitler. His philosophy was to be ready for the worst case.

The operation is circular, as he put it. First a foreign holding company, then a cash transfer into it. With this money, the holding company purchases Concordia shares, the house, anything it likes, while paying for whatever it purchases into an account abroad held to the owner's name. Chasing your own tail, except that the factory ownership and the fortune ended up outside the country, with luck protected from events. Of course there was no need to live anywhere else but

Pernsdorf. His German clients, however, were in an altogether more constricting and difficult position. Shell companies were to be acquired for the purpose through the good offices of his friend Senor Ruiz-Ordonez, of the Venezuelan legation in Berlin. Sure, Senor Ruiz-Ordonez accepted an honorarium but his government approved of the whole collaboration so long as confidentiality was respected.

'Take precautions,' Rex urged her. 'Send for this man, even if nothing comes of it.'

Senor Ruiz-Ordonez suffered from the climate of central Europe. Winter was too cold for him, summer too hot. Though hardly forty, he carried a walking-stick. Nobody could have been more polite. Venezuela and its neutrality, he assured them, enjoyed the respect of the whole world. A range of suitably structured companies was available, each duly registered and certified. Instructions had only to be given. Of course his legation approved of the procedures he was recommending, the national interest could only benefit.

'And we have to trust them,' Henriette said, 'the North American hippo, the South American crab.'

Rex did not leave it alone. The office had to check out the New York law firm in which Chester Warren was a partner; take soundings at South American legations in Vienna. A planning session was arranged at Concordia. In the event of war in Europe, Eduard von Arnheim conceded, the factory would be exposed, its output certainly diverted to exclusively military purposes. The intentions of statesmen were at about the same doubtful level as lawyers' ideas.

'I want nothing out of this for myself,' Rex assured Henriette, 'I'm doing what I can because Rudi isn't here, Margulies is no longer up to it, Eduard has no imagination. One day it may be too late. You saw the storm-troopers for yourself.'

That summer, Jules was again in Greece, travelling with Quappi Verwey. His twenty-first birthday would have been celebrated at Pernsdorf in November, if the row had not intervened.

Plans had existed in outline for several months, Henriette

told him, to transfer the ownership of the factory into a foreign holding.

As a share-holder, he replied, he had had a right to be consulted earlier. How could anyone have confidence in what was being proposed? What evidence of good faith was there? Then he asked Rex to leave the room.

'Everything you have to say may be said to his face. I absolutely forbid him to leave.'

'Poor Henny,' said Rex, but he walked away all the same.

The most dramatic of Henriette's night-rages followed. Was it not her generosity that had given him shares in the first place? Ingratitude, vanity, insubordination, the reproaches rolled like thunder in her head. Much too much had been done for the boy, he had been spoiled because he had made a nuisance of himself; she should never have listened to Professor Warschawsky and Benies-Granadia who had forced her into making every allowance for his behaviour. Sleep was out of the question; self-pity stormed within her. In the service of father, husband and son, she had worn herself out. Prematurely grey and aged, she had never indulged her own tastes, and now here was her reward, to be alone in the small hours, the pillow wet with tears, a pain in her chest.

It was mid-morning before she ordered the maid to summon Jules. Haggard, in the false calm of utter fatigue, she lay back with a satin wrap around her night-dress. Jules knocked. Under the chair on which he was ordered to sit were her slippers, also of satin, with high heels.

'In my own house,' she began, 'I will not be told what I may or may not do.'

'Money will pass out of your control at some stage, into the hands of these people. What proof is there that it will be returned?'

'I am a widow, in case you have not noticed. I am defenceless. Nobody thinks of me. Rex is trying only to protect me.'

'An ex-schoolmaster actually, from an absolutely obscure private school in England. Without the least experience of business or finance or law.' And no protector at that, in fact something very different, not really a man at all – *everyone knew that*, Jules said, *the whole of Vienna was laughing.*

Another knock on the door, and Rex entered

'I shall be leaving this house as soon as possible.'

'If anyone is to leave, it will be Jules who does not understand what a son owes his mother.'

So strange and complex is human fate that the confrontation between three highly-strung personalities proved not to be emotional indulgence, but a matter of life and death.

In the irrationality of anger, Henriette put Chester Warren's scheme into practice. Once again, in the interest of Concordia, she mobilised her resources. The money to be paid into the holding company had to be untraceable. Bundles of notes, collected by Eduard von Arnheim and Margulies, lay on the floor of the office, to be counted and recounted, compressed into packets with elastic bands, wrapped in newspaper. The suitcase into which this money was placed had belonged to Rudi, and hotel labels were stuck brightly on to its sides. Przeweck drove them to the legation, with the suitcase on the back seat. Burschen Franz's son, Heinz, was not informed what it was that he was supposed to be escorting. In Vienna by special appointment, Senor Ruiz-Ordonez had hay-fever on that day, and was snuffling into a silk handkerchief. Lawyers were already present. The documents to be signed had been printed on a pale grey paper of a quality so poor that the ink ran and smudged. Caracas Metals S.A. came into existence, with Concordia as its principal asset. Accounts were opened in that name in London and in Zurich in the bank where Baron Gustav had always kept his fortune. The sole signature was Henriette's. A member of the legation staff carried the suitcase out of the room.

Their intention was to go to Zurich, and then London, where Chester Warren would meet them, claiming his fee on the conclusion of the whole process of the transfer. Last-minute details delayed them. The Lecomte-du-Nouy had developed cracks in the paintwork. This was an opportunity to send the picture to Grollnitzer, the restorer. Not since it had first been hung had it been lowered ; five men carried it out to a van. After the departure of the Arab prince and his retinue, the hall became ordinary, almost drab.

Mysteriously a stranger arrived. The man was perspiring with agitation and haste. Word had spread within the Jewish community, he said, that the Baronin was emigrating, and he had been delegated to secure the papers of her grandfather, Professor Dreinach. He hoped that he was not too late. Nobody had so thoroughly researched tribal origins in the Dark Ages ; material in the archives might fortify the Jewish position.

'The rumour is ridiculous. We have no intention of emigrating.'

'With my own eyes I can see your preparations. Your pictures seem to be packed already. And your industrial concerns ... We must secure our culture.'

'The papers are as Professor Pollner and his assistant last left them. Nobody touches them. You may have access after our return, you or whoever you nominate. We expect to be here from April onwards.'

Henriette and Rex were in London when the Austrian crisis was precipitated, the plebiscite was announced, Chancellor Schuschnigg was summoned to Berchtesgaden. So it happened that on 13 March 1938 the news of the German take-over of Austria was broken to them by a Piccadilly newsboy. Opposite their hotel was a cinema in which they watched Gaumont and Pathé news-reels of Hitler himself in Vienna, inspecting his troops in the Heldenplatz, emerging on the balcony of the very same suite in the Imperial where Gustav had lived with Else after their marriage. Later a call came from Jules to say that he and Quappi Verwey were safe in Budapest, and would probably go to Sagodvar.

So it came about that on that day Burschen Franz and his son Heinz slipped away across the park, and into the city.

On that day too, Amelie was free to cram two suitcases full of Henriette's clothes, and to help herself to a fur-coat, and leave these things with her sister before joining the rest of the population jubilantly waving and cheering and welcoming

Hitler and the German army in the occupation of the city.

So it came about that Baron Gustav's house stood in the dark, and not a single light was switched on.

·Twenty Six·

'I went straight back on the Orient Express' (in Rex's version of events). 'Grinning louts thumbing your passport. The place had become unrecognisable, it could as well have been Baghdad. No Prizzy-Wizzy waiting that time, but that's beside the point. It was the faces on the streets which made the impression. The swastikas and the yelling and marching about, you could tell yourself, were really rather childish, but there was nothing the least childish about those faces. Where had they been hiding themselves until then? The wand had been waved and they'd been transformed. One woman in a shop swore she wouldn't serve me until I said Heil Hitler. All that stuff and nonsense about their great culture, their music and poetry, it wasn't even skin-deep. The animal was right there.

'When he heard I was in the house, Burschen Franz came round. It was a sad sight. We packed up what we could. I ordered a lorry round from the factory, with the carpenters. Fourteen crates in all. Quite tidy. Personal property of Captain Smail-Turner. The British embassy was useless, didn't want to know. Far too busy making sure that nothing and nobody upset Herr Hitler. Our Venezuelan friends came to the rescue. The South Americans were together in the racket, a load was already booked to leave under the auspices of the Dominican Republic. The diplomatic bag was a euphemism for a whole sealed train. Hundreds of families had that chance to save themselves and their things. It wasn't cheap. Getting the money out before the Anschluss was nothing compared to the cost of those crates.

'In the crates were the portraits of her parents which Henriette had always kept by her bed, her jewel-case and her vanity-case, the best of the Chinese lacquer boxes, Else's pearls, Kismet's mounted horse-shoe, family albums and mementoes, the photographs of Henriette on her eighteenth birthday and of Jules by C.Pietzner, some valuable books, carpets, silver including Baron Gustav's monogrammed forks and spoons, the pair of candlesticks once given to her by Rudi.

'Henny's household gods, sacred stuff, for heaven's sake I'd been living there long enough to know what was what. Property of Captain Smail-Turner, address in Ciudad Rodrigo, in letters a foot high on the crates. Actually the consignment was off-loaded in Rotterdam, we had it shipped from there. We had to spend a day at Dover when the customs refused to believe it was all the property of a gentleman. Trust them. For weeks we feared we were facing a bill for import duty.'

Leo Margulies and his wife, both in their eighties, swallowed cyanide. Benies-Granadia reached New York, only to commit suicide there.

Rudi's parents fled to their daughter in Czechoslovakia. None of them survived the war. Leviseur was seen scrubbing pavements. After the ordeal he was sent to a concentration camp and disappeared.

Responsibility for the Waisenhaus was assumed by Adolf Eichmann, then still a middle-ranking Party official, an Austrian by birth. Eichmann's task was to apply the Nuremberg laws, and in particular to curb the independence of Jewish institutions. For the purpose, he exploited the Kultusgemeinde, or governing council of the Jewish community. The orphans were evacuated to a Kultusgemeinde home. In the first winter of the war, Dr Ostersetzer died of pleurisy. Frau Ostersetzer was posted to a hospital in Graz set aside for Jews too infirm and old to be deported but certain to die shortly from natural causes.

'What would have happened to us?' Henriette asks. 'Without Rex, I should have been lost.'

'I only did what anyone would have done.'

As early as 26 March 1938, in a speech at the Nordwestbahnhalle about the economic prospects for the Greater Reich incorporating Austria, or the Ostmark as it was designated, Hermann Goering mentioned Concordia as an example of an enterprise of strategic potential whose Jewish ownership could not be tolerated. In the initial measures of 'aryanisation', Bürckel, the Gauleiter of Vienna, appointed a civil commissioner with special powers to take over, sequestrate or otherwise administer private Jewish assets. Among the commissioner's personnel was a Dr Huber, with the rank of *Hauptsturmführer*, and holding a *Diplomvolkswirt*, a degree approved by the Party, from Hamburg university. Dr Huber preferred to wear a suit rather than a uniform. A technician, a professional, he determined to prove that he could control Pernsdorf and the vacated orphanage on the Dornbacherstrasse and the factory quite as efficiently as if he were Baron Ellingen himself.

Party nominees under Dr Huber were appointed to the Concordia board. Eduard von Arnheim, Dr Verelst and Dr Loebel took their place among them. Lawyers turned their attention to undoing the transfer of ownership into Caracas Metals. The solution was for the Party nominees to issue new majority share-holdings to themselves, and then to vote in their own right to merge Concordia into the gigantic Hermann-Goering-Werke, the corporate structure which effectively controlled the output of iron and steel in the Third Reich. Even so, Baldur von Schirach, Bürckel's successor as Gauleiter, thought fit to pass a decree retroactively annulling as illegal and void all measures taken since 1933 which might be considered 'to have the aim of diminishing, impairing, expatriating or otherwise sabotaging the indivisible German patrimony.'

'How many times I wrote to Jules, I poured my heart out' (in Henriette's version of events), 'I implored and beseeched. Everything was changed. Cruelly as he had treated Rex and me, I had long since forgiven him, though I could never forget it. His head was in the clouds. No idea of the real world. As a child, he'd push facts aside to suit his imagination. To be at Sagodvar was like being wrapped in cotton wool. How was he to realise what others were going through? What a lovely place that was. He was like a little king there. After Quappi Verwey, he fell in love with Litzi Seideler, from Budapest. Why should he have left? I suppose he believed himself safe. The von Pechys proved true friends, they intervened with the *gendarmerie* at Gyor to obtain a residence permit for him.

'Yes, I also wrote when Rex and I were married. We half-expected him to turn up at the last minute at the St Pancras Town Hall. That would have been typical. The registrar was a woman, she was wearing a hat practically identical to mine, grey felt, we both burst out laughing. 24 May 1938, it would still have been easy for Jules to climb aboard any train and come over to us. Rex could have arranged it with the Home Office, naturalisation or whatever. We were renting a flat near Regent's Park at that point, while searching for somewhere permanent in the country. But he never arrived.'

Before 1939, and for a while after, Hungary was relatively tranquil, though not quite 'wrapped in cotton wool' as Henriette says. Admiral Horthy, the Regent, believed that in the end the democracies would prevail over both Germany and the Soviet Union. His prime ministers, however, notably Daranyi and Imredy, were prepared to appease Hitler to gain a short-term advantage, and in that respect it was expedient to move against the Jews. When political and military developments were to bring Hungary into the war on the German side, the fate of Jews in that country was sealed.

Jules neither waited on events nor tried to escape. On the contrary, towards the end of March or early in April 1941, he chose instead to return to Austria. Whatever his motives were, he kept them to himself. Arrested at the frontier, he was taken to Vienna and held in the Gestapo headquarters on the Morzinplatz. Deported, at some unknown date between his twenty-fifth and twenty-sixth birthdays, he became one of the victims of mass-murder.

Twenty Seven

Marietta Carrassi (née Revertella) to Henriette, 1 June 1945 :

You may imagine the emotion with which I recognised your writing on the envelope. Hardly a day has passed when I did not think of you or speak about you, in hope for your well-being, and wondering if past times would ever return. Now we know that nothing can ever again be what it was. Rather than sink under grief and mourning, we must cultivate hope. We stand at the opening of quite another period, which cannot be worse than what we have experienced.

The complex personality of Jules did not allow him easily to admit to happiness but I am sure that at Sagodvar in those last years he was as happy as he could be. How he used to camouflage his emotions. Under that apologetic half-smile was great self-confidence and strength, a sort of bed-rock of character. In the summer before the war, I was there, and the old hectic life was going on just the same. Franz Pidoll, Nettie, Irma Grunberger, Professor Reischl, how to make contact with them I don't yet know but there must be some in our little circle who will bear out what I say. Toni tried to bring us down to earth. Precisely because for a short span he himself had fervently believed in Hitler, he sounded the warning. They would stop at nothing, he said, he had seen the military preparations with his own eyes. Once the war started, he insisted that we had to force on to Jules the realities and dangers of the position. But it wasn't until the last week-end of October 1940 that we were able to make time for the journey there together.

I remember the date exactly because the meeting had just occurred between Hitler and Pétain, the French were deciding on collaboration. We had always looked to France, listening to the wireless we were stunned. Nobody could think how Hitler would be beaten but we refused to believe that he could rule the whole continent for the rest of our lives.

You could blame Litzi Seideler for his behaviour, but in my

honest opinion this would be mistaken. She was very much in love, I have no doubt, but she was also independent, not the clinging type. I would think it inconceivable that he returned to Vienna either to be rid of her or to hurt her in some destructive way. That was not how I saw him or their relationship. I liked her very much, and you would have liked her too. She had extraordinary appeal, and if anything a calming effect on him.

Quite clearly I can recall Toni asking him what he thought was happening inside Austria, what our friends were facing. Specifically, why not try to escape while there was still a chance? For a long time he sat in silence with his hands pressing on his cheeks. He despised running away. The opposite, rather, was to be involved. At the centre of his decision to return, I believe, was a longing to go through the experience of his people. It was an adventure, for want of a better word, which he felt he owed himself. Does that make sense to you? At the time, of course, nobody foresaw that it would end in martyrdom. If anyone lived with despair it was not Jules but Toni. I am enclosing the last photograph we had of him, taken in the desert by a friend in his regiment. To me, the cigarette drooping on his lip in an act of pure defiance, it is the cigarette handed out as a last gesture by the executioner and smoked with indifference to his face. Poor Toni, to have to find such pride in his death.

Louise von Arnheim, to Henriette, 13 June 1945 :

Let me ask you, with all respect to our old love and affection for one another, what did we survive for? Nothing in the world will bring back Jules or my Eduard. Transferred to Augsburg, to the aircraft factories, Eduard died there in 1943. Did we survive in order to have no more tears to shed? It is not quite eight weeks since Wasserburg was destroyed when a party of soldiers refused to surrender. Utterly burnt out, the house was the final casualty of the war. Except for the clothes on my back, I have nothing. Had friends not taken me under their roof I would have had nowhere to turn. A few years ago, if anyone had predicted what we now take for granted, I should have dismissed him as a lunatic. Now we are learning the full wickedness and madness of the Nazis. We suffered their daily abuses, but never for a minute could we have suspected what they were doing in their insane secrecy. When we meet at last, I shall tell you all I know. It was in the summer of 1941, July or August at the latest, that we heard rumours that Jules was in the hands of the

Gestapo. At first we wondered whether he had been kidnapped, or somehow tricked. Eduard consulted with Dr Huber, the commissioner, with whom we were on quite correct terms. Huber told him that Jules had returned of his own free will, they had picked him up at Sopron, crossing over. It seems that he told them that he wanted to be at Pernsdorf. Then we heard that he would be sent to the east for resettlement.

Huber was not the worst of them. Wooden, pedantic, but he managed your properties as though he himself were the rightful owner. Americans are at Pernsdorf, the Russians at the factory. Please waste no time in coming out, you may be able to salvage remnants, though it is second nature for those of us here to be constantly afraid of what may happen. My whole life seems to pass futilely before my eyes as I sink and drown in this misery.

Prince Paul Solkovsky, to Henriette, 2 October 1945 :

Our two families have been indissolubly linked. My father was the first to acknowledge his indebtedness to Baron Gustav. I too remember your father with admiration, and dare I say it, familiarity. You and your late husband were generosity itself to me. This is all the more reason for the deep contrition with which I address you now.

Moreover I was brought up a devout Christian, taught that the doctrines of the church are not mere words but precepts upon which our actions must be founded.

So confused have my feelings been, that until lately I had thought to suppress what I am about to describe to you. You would never find out, I told myself, and besides, I too was a victim of circumstances. These and other rationalisations are specious and inadequate. Silence, I learn, is complicity. Only confession will enable me to extract myself from German guilt, to come to terms with the contribution I have made to hatefulness. The fact that there was no positive course of action that I could have taken is no alleviation. In atoning through this letter, I will not abase you by asking for pardon, that in itself will reveal a dimension of spirit to which, in all conscience, I have no claim, no right.

The fact is that I was vouchsafed a sight of Jules. He was a prisoner. This is how it happened. For the first years of the war, I managed to be stationed in the Sudetenland close to Rentzenburg. In view of my age, I had succeeded in avoiding active service. That I was a staff officer with the 117th Infantry Division was in good measure due to a friend of mine, General Schaer. He had served on the Eastern front and had seen for himself what the SS did in the wake of the Wehrmacht. On his return he had been decorated by Hitler in person, and they had shaken hands. As a result, he told me, he felt polluted, and he went so far as to add that anyone who shook his hand now risked the same pollution. We Germans should realize what was being done in our name, he insisted, for surely we should be held accountable.

For that reason, he and I and two other like-minded staff-officers drove in a staff car the eighty or so kilometres from our barracks to Theresienstadt. This was in the middle of November 1941, when the place was already notorious as a clearing-station for deportations to the East. Snow was beginning to fall as we drove through the forests. The old fortress had been converted into a ghetto, and it was already afternoon when we decided to tour it. A column of prisoners marched past. In ordinary clothes for the most part, they could not have survived the winter for long. We fully realized that fact. Looking at them, I recognised Jules. I had only to reach out to have touched his shoulder. Our eyes met. I am certain that he recognised me, his gaze seemed to linger, to burn in my direction. As the column receded, I stood rooted to the spot, hoping to convince myself that the man was someone else, and not the companion of my childhood. News had reached me that he had been on your estates in Hungary, and I had supposed him to have escaped to England or America. To leave that place was a complete surrender, but already General Schaer and the others were stamping their feet and rubbing their hands, grumbling about the cold. In spite of the frankness that existed between us as brother officers, I dared not confide to the general what had just happened. Nothing that I could have done would have changed the fate of Jules or the entire column of unfortunates, for that matter, but that is not an answer to the look he gave me. In what spirit, and for how long, I must ask my conscience, did the sight of my face and my uniform remain in his memory?

Twenty Eight

From the windows of the bus, Pernsdorf village looked unchanged : the cobbled square with a drinking fountain at its centre, two green-grocers, the *gasthaus*. Not since childhood, in the company of Guffy, had Henriette travelled out by means of public transport, and then only as an exceptional treat. Morning mist had dampened windows, shop-fronts, branches, pavements. Low cloud, with rain in it, prevented the sun breaking through.

At the lodge the iron gates were missing ; that was the first thing she saw. Instead, a temporary barrier had been laid across the drive with a sign, No Entry, Out of Bounds. Beyond was her house, with its stonework and timbering, the windows blank, with the steep slate pitch and turrets and pepper-pots a sombre mass against the watery grey of the sky. The next thing she noticed was that the ancestral copper-beech had been cut down. That tree had been in the background when she had been photographed on her eighteenth birthday with her father and the retainers. The stump, like a scar turned septic, glistened in the grass which was strewn around with mouldering saw-dust and shavings.

She climbed the terrace steps where weeds now were growing ragged. The house was open, deserted. Through the glass dome above the hall the light was its familiar diffused and obscure yellow. Even after that lapse of time, the outline of the picture-frame of the Arab prince remained imprinted against the back of the stairwell. A long and jagged scorch-mark had been blazed on the parquet flooring, where a fire had been lit.

'War damages, most certainly,' the official at the Foreign Office had told her. 'We are establishing a Compensation

Committee for British subjects. Claims for the factory, claims for the house, of course. We shall need whatever records you can provide, title-deeds, inventories, balance sheets, schedules of investments. We intend to pursue the matter of compensation with utmost vigour.'

'You must allow a period of time,' the lawyers agreed, 'your claims will have to be sifted, weighed against other claimants and priorities.'

That was how they spoke in London, far away from the reality of the house stripped down to bare plaster and boards. In the drawing-room, as in the dining-room, the fire-places in massive Tolentino marble had been prised out. Not even fitted shelving remained in the library. In Margulies's office, several of the floor-boards had been broken away. Jules's billiard table had gone.

She climbed the stairs, to the room where she had been born, and which she had occupied for the best part of her life. No panelling, no shutters, no doors : dust everywhere. The plumbing and even the wiring had been hacked out of the walls.

Standing there, she heard footsteps, then someone shouting.

'Who the hell are you ? Natives aren't allowed in here.'

The American sergeant hauling himself up the stairs was so fat that he appeared to roll from side to side as he hurried towards her. His uniform was stretched at the buttons. He spoke with the butt of an unlit cigar in his mouth.

They considered moving in, this sergeant explained, but other places were more suitable. Some home, said the sergeant. He and his men were quartered out at the back in the stables, they had transport, they'd be glad to drive her back.

But first she went with the sergeant to the upper floors, to the corridors where Jules had invented his obstacle course, to the turret where he had had his piano, to the nursery, to the room where her grandfather's papers had been stored and in which there was nothing but a solitary scrap to be picked off the floor : an advertisement for ready-made curtains in synthetic fabrics torn from a 1943 newspaper.

In years to come, there would be some who asked her what the return to her past had been like. 'I was glad to find the sergeant,' was the reply. 'I made a deep impression when I got out of their three-tonner at the hotel, the doorman could hardly believe his eyes.'

In years to come, the reunion with Louise von Arnheim was also buried under the weight of emotion. The address for Louise was in a part of the city into which she had never before penetrated, in streets seemingly in perpetual shadow as the houses reared high above them, one tenement building after another. Liver-coloured brick, with a bewildering variety of doorways and stairs and landings on which were communal basins with a single cold-water tap.

What should I see on entering but my own things, Henriette would say, my Augarten china, my Alt-Wien, glasses with the Ellingen monogram on them, the little marquetry table of my father's, even firedogs from the library.

She never told me. Which was neither honest nor straightforward. Why not have written with the good news about what she had saved? Because she had stolen all of it, and never suspected that I might catch her red-handed using my things in that flat. She'd imagined that we would be meeting in the hotel. So don't talk to me of those people, that's what they are like.

'Do I deny what is yours? what am I hiding?'

At Wasserburg, there had been plenty more. Whole loads rescued from the house while Dr Huber's back was turned – whole loads now burnt to ashes.

The grievances of the two women were less with one another than with events outside their control. Nonetheless the words were formed, and in them were passions that neither could forgive. In years to come, Louise wrote letters, and they were returned to her unopened.

'Ask Heinz if I stole anything, I had him help me fetch and carry. He knows.'

And the interview with Heinz took place in Sacher's Hotel, where Henriette was staying because the Imperial was still requisitioned and the suite once her father's inhabited by a

Red Army man. Opposite her hotel room lay the ruined masonry of the opera house, and further away the rubble of the Jockey Club.

Heinz's pre-war suit was too large for his frame. His hair was still shaved right up above his ears, military-style. Conscripted into the Wehrmacht, he told Henriette, he had been stationed in Normandy, at Evreux, on the commissariat staff. Those were the days, when he and the farmers had been the best of friends. What meals! Regular feasts, washed down with Calvados. Until there had been an accident, a lorry backed and pinned him against a wall, crushing his shoulder. So he had been invalided home, and had managed never to return to active service. Which was fine, except that he was handicapped still today, and no chance of work. Not like his poor late father. Sixty years, a life-time, in the service of the family.

'And what was stolen from the house?'

'Stealing, Frau Baronin, is one thing, the war was another. Amelie took clothes, to be sure, and your fur-coats. With respect, she went off saying that we could be sure Jews would never be seen around here again. What's happened to Przeweck I have no idea. Have you noticed already, Frau Baronin, that nobody was a Nazi? It makes you wonder how it all happened. Dr Huber, now, he was a Party man, but a gentleman, better than many who are saying they were anti-Nazi. He did his best. Live and let live. Yes, I helped Frau von Arnheim, we removed quite a bit to Wasserburg, but I had nothing to do with the cognac.'

'The cognac?'

'After the Director-General died in Germany, she had nobody to support her. It was desperate. The cellar at the back, nobody else knew Baron Gustav's cognac was there, we had the only keys. Very old, those cases, and worth a fortune. She sold them, she said you would surely let her have them if you had realised her situation.'

In years to come, Henriette used to say that she had learned the meaning of hate, in the grip of claustrophobia, in solitude and rage, desiring never to hear the German language again, never to encounter anyone who spoke it, staring at the ruins outside the window. They already had Jules, let them have house and factory, past and future.

And it was in that moment of eclipse, of break-down as she later called it, that the telephone rang and the concierge was on the line in answer to a previous request of hers. Finally he had succeeded in tracking down the information about Grollnitzer the restorer. A bomb had scored a direct hit on the place, Grollnitzer himself had been killed outright, all the pictures in storage had quite definitely been burned, and if one of hers had been among them then that was that. To corroborate the facts, he had the names and addresses of two or three men, including someone from the Kunsthistorisches Museum.

'Oh come come, Mrs Smail-Turner,' said the colonel at the British Military Mission, 'We'll lay on transport for you, we mustn't let ourselves be down-hearted because central Europe is rather ropey right now. We'd be delighted to help you reach your Hungarian property.'

She telegraphed to Sagodvar. 'Do not travel, conditions unsettled,' the reply stated, 'we will come to you.' And so they did, Egyedy and his daughter Margit. In the ground floor *salon* of Sacher's, on a plush-lined bench under a chandelier without light-bulbs or candles in it, they told her that the house was intact, the village undamaged. More than that: Jules had lived with a girl called Litzi Seideler, she had had a baby, and just before the Nazis came to deport her, she had managed to leave that baby with them at Sagodvar.

·Part Three·

·*Twenty Nine*·

I am Julius, the child of Litzi Seideler and Jules Hechter.

At times my picture of them is so clear that we might be in the room together – the French windows are open, lime pollen sweetens the air, and Litzi stretches on a sofa. I see her brown eyes and hair, she favours clothes of a huntsman's green in the country. A belt with a shiny clasp shows off her waist. The muscles of her calves are as india-rubber – proof of serious and disciplined work. She reads Maupassant, cries easily, mislays her handbag, acts the *ingénue*. Always vivacious movements ; a brush of the hand across her face, a twitch of a smile, the stiffening of sinews in a beautiful neck when she turns her head to look at starlings suddenly squabbling on the terrace. Jules stands with his hands in his pockets. In the grate behind him, the split birch logs are tidy, and will lie there all summer. The walls are covered with the pictures of race-horses. A man in his own house. No tie, an English knitted sweater with a pattern on it, bright socks, yellow perhaps or cream-coloured, and brogues. He has an impatient manner, he wants something to happen, his mouth droops except when he is laughing. He raises his voice. She murmurs, she keeps the peace. The talk is about guests and plans, a visit to Budapest, night-clubs, dancing in the village, and gypsy music.

Only a few years old, I am playing with toys on the carpet, under the eye of a nanny, another Guffy, in a starched uniform. I am also due to ride on the train with Pista the mechanic, I will be allowed to blow the whistle, we shall have a picnic under the willows along the frothy stream winding towards Zalaszentistvan. I am taken out to learn how to handle my first gun, and the partridge I bring home has feet like dry gristle, its blood in a curve of a smear on the back of my hand. Litzi hugs me with pride.

Or I am at the age I have actually reached, looking coolly at my mother, this woman who never grows older, this woman without a wrinkle whom I see so intimately but who does not speak to me. The day-dream of this existence goes on and on, and we are suspended in it and there is no war.

'They arrived at the hotel,' Henriette has told me a hundred times. 'They stood there staring at me. Like a pair of owls. Remember that I hadn't seen Egyedy since before the war, and Margit had been at the pig-tail stage then. I had no idea how they had been managing. Inflation was destroying the currency, you needed millions to buy anything, Sagodvar satisfied daily needs, but what about a tractor or a harvester? "That's what I was worrying about, Frau Baronin," poor Egyedy said to me. "We saw Jules just before he went to the station. He left in good faith." That was their phrase. He thought he could do something, save the house and factory, talk to Huber the resident gauleiter. And he ditched Litzi. That was unintentional. You were already born when Litzi returned to Sagodvar. The Germans were deporting everybody, all through the summer of forty-four.'

Quite another Litzi walks before me. A woman in a shabby unbuttoned coat, flat shoes, a woman with a gaunt face, carrying in her arms a baby. Between the station and the house, she keeps to side-lanes which are muddy. Rainwater gleams in the pot-holes. A clammy April wind is blowing. Nobody is about but peasants will have watched her. She knows the back entrance here, through the dog cemetery, past the stables, with the gardens on her right. No flowers now, no clipped shrubs and hedges. She peers through a window. Saddles and harness have already disappeared from the estate office. A small man, Egyedy stands with his legs apart, accentuating the paunch – he puts his energies into everything, meals included. He is in breeches and gaiters, too harassed to concentrate, shaking his head, irritated by the baby's crying. Piri Egyedy rubs her hands on an apron, tells Margit to stop listening to things which are none of her business. A moment of truth :

are they or are they not going to accept this burden? Behind curtains, the peasants observe that Litzi is alone on the way back to the provincial station with its once-white railings. Nobody knows whether such a thing as a train time-table still exists, but they see how Litzi stretches out on a bench to wait. And that journey prefigures another, only weeks later, also without a schedule. Why the shabby coat, I ask myself, the flat shoes?

For eighteen months I was at Sagodvar, they tell me; the only member of the family, the last member of the family to live there. I cannot be sure of my one recollection of it. I am out of doors, squatting close to grass, and cramming something into my mouth: gravel? a bone, perhaps? I am prevented, I am astonished by the sudden tug of anger on my arm.

'You couldn't find a car for love or money,' Henriette says. 'I walked with the Egyedys for miles, they were staying with relations of theirs. My feet were a mass of blisters. Russian patrols pointed a gun at us to make us step off the pavements. You never said a word. You stared at me without expression, pushing out your lower lip, as much as to say, what's this? Jules was the same at that age.'

Rex joined her. 'He was wonderful,' Henriette says. 'All those months he never complained.'

There was also a journey to Switzerland, to her bank in Zurich. Her own accounts were in order. In Jules's case, the law required a death certificate in due form, from Auschwitz if that was where he had been murdered. In its absence, the assets remained frozen, could not be released even to next-of-kin. A pity, the lawyers agreed, but where would the banks be if the dead were to appear to claim what was theirs?

'I lay in bed,' Henriette says, 'and couldn't move. I ate only chocolate. Strange what you remember. All through the war we hadn't seen even silver paper. We were being punished because he had been murdered. The banks made themselves accessories. There was no arguing with them. And the whole thing began again in Vienna. It was a nightmare. I called you Julius naturally but how was I to prove who you were? The High Commission, the Military Mission, the Red Cross, the refugee people, I saw them all. I wrote to members of parliament, and applied to the Home Office. We had Christmas in the hotel, our first Christmas together.'

A newspaper cutting exists with the head-line, 'Grandmother's Agony Reclaiming Lost Family'. The woman quotes me saying, 'I want to go home.' That must be fiction. I knew no English.

In 1946, when we travelled to England together, Henriette was fifty-four.

'You must have been three, or four at the most,' Henriette always says, 'Baron Gustav set you a precedent when it comes to dates of birth. Do you know, you hardly spoke at all on the journey, not even when you saw the Channel, and you wouldn't let anyone so much as hold your hand.'

·*Thirty*·

Henriette's home is called Perry's Ridge. A local paint manufacturer built the house between the wars and sold it when his
wife died unexpectedly. Under a clear Home Counties sky the
brick is a friendly red, but rain seems to darken this colour
rather forbiddingly to purple. The tiles on the roof are square,
unusually thick and old-fashioned. A short gravel drive leads
straight to the front door, and from there sweeps around in a
circle behind the house. Front and back are expanses of lawn,
which Rex worked so hard to maintain. The surrounding
woods are something of a screen. Every so often the trees are
thinned for hop-poles, which makes for easier walking to the
village. Five minutes downhill, but more like a quarter of an
hour up, for the house is actually built on the top of a ridge.

Mr and Mrs Smail-Turner : who would guess what lay
behind the double-barrelled mouthful ? Like the paint manufacturer, what they must have wanted was a conventional life
in the country. Only quite lately have I been able to realise
what an upheaval the arrival of a small child must have been.

Rex, as I knew him, was handsome ; the man had presence.
The back was straight, the eyes blue and bright, the hair a distinguished grey-white. When he smiled or laughed, however,
the wide mouth opened to reveal teeth which were small and
stained, teeth which made an old man of him. Gardener's
hands, big, blunt, strong – but on one little finger he wore a
signet-ring which I afterwards knew had belonged to Rudi,
and on the other a blue band, enamel or opaline perhaps,
which suddenly feminised the whole appearance. Unless he
had some reason to dress up, he never wore a tie, but preferred
to knot a silk scarf round his throat. Corduroys and a cardigan
in winter, linen trousers and short-sleeved shirt in summer.

My room in Perry's Ridge is under the roof, with a dormer window and a view over the tree-tops, with the village below, and at night the lights in houses like stars in the valley. Until I came, suitcases had been stored here, the suitcases once used to bring possessions from Pernsdorf. Henriette, who never could bring herself to throw anything away, cleared the lot out for me. On the floor below, Henriette and Rex had separate rooms. From the beginning, I was made to understand that neither of them could bear the least noise upstairs, and I would not be forgiven for waking them up. On their floor was also the spare room, with the bathroom which I was allowed to use. The stairs, especially the third and fourth treads, creaked and until it almost hurt I used to postpone what might be the crime of creeping down to a lavatory that had to be flushed. Was there more of a risk in the glare of the hundred-watt bulb overhead, or in stubbing a toe in the dark on the uncarpeted wooden boards?

'I insisted that the Hen collect you,' Rex said. 'Believe me, we were delighted. You can't remember that first Christmas in the hotel in Vienna, but she was a changed woman. Something had been saved from the war, and that something was you.'

The cigarette in his hand was held in a deliberately uninvolved way, as if it had nothing to do with him. Finishing it, he liked to cough. The chest will get me in the end, he would say, with a look almost of pleasure on his face.

'The Boy will make you stop,' Henriette said one day, 'Go on, you order him.'

So I did.

'He'd stop me dead in my tracks. The Boy's got killer eyes.'

Those killer eyes – years were to pass before I had any conception of what he might mean. The expression had staying-power, though, just like The Boy, his nickname for me. Sometimes he called me Killer-eyes.

'But I don't have killer eyes.'

'There's a good chap, just ribbing.'

Perhaps I still do not appreciate that the language I was acquiring was modelled on that of an Edwardian, the type who went to music-halls and filled his speech with quips and tags and bits of slang. 'Trip the light fantastic,' he might say, no matter whether it had any meaning in the context or merely filled a pause in the conversation, or drop some favourite jingle like 'Roses are red, violets are blue, I'm an ass and so are you.' How boring our lessons must have been to him. It was a danger signal that I could recognise when he started to hum, 'Nymphs and shepherds come away,' ending with a languid repetition of 'Come come come come away ...' Most of this sort of humour, and especially the irony in it, escaped me but for hours he could keep it up, bobbing up and down on the charm of his chatter like a swimmer on a calm sea.

By nine o'clock in the morning he was downstairs in his dressing-gown, sitting with a cup of coffee, and with Robbie, the labrador, at his feet. An hour or more passed while he read the newspapers. A flurry of activity meant that Miss Butley had arrived for the house-work. An hour or ninety minutes could then be fitted in before lunch to spend time with me, principally teaching me English, spoken and written. On the card-table he laid out sheets of paper and ruled wide parallel lines on them, between which I was supposed to form pothook letters. From his newspapers I began to spell out words in large type. 'I'll larn the Boy,' he liked to encourage, 'I wasn't a schoolmaster in my hey-day for nothing.' And later, addressing me in the third person as if speaking about someone else, 'I larned him well, didn't I? And he's a good Boy, ain't he?'

The drawing-room runs the length of the house. At either end is a picture window. The fire-place in the middle has been blocked in, fitted with the pre-war kind of electric heater, consisting of three bars behind a chrome safety grille. To switch on any one of those bars is to catch a whiff of suddenly singed dust – that is the smell of my childhood. The matching sofas are chintz-covered. Beyond them stands the card-table, with ash trays built into each corner. At heart, Henriette is indifferent to decoration. The colours she chooses are fawn and cream and beige. The dining-room opposite is a chill yellow. Rather than create a setting of her own, Henriette has formalised the past through material objects. Everything from Pernsdorf has its ordained place and role. Photographs : of Henriette's mother in her silk dress at the time of her engagement ; of Henriette herself, at Concordia with her father and Minister Chlumecky, and on her own eighteenth birthday among her retainers ; of Jules, artistically posed in the studio of C.Pietzner. On the mantelpiece above the thin strips of the electric heater in its asbestos surround are the candlesticks of noble savages, black and ormulu, he with his bow and arrow, she with her parrot. On the wall hangs the picture of Kismet, groomed to perfection. The silver forks and spoons carry Baron Gustav's monogram. On the side-board stands the samovar for hot water, once laid out for tea by Burschen Franz. Chinese lacquer boxes have survived, and the writing-case, several albums, and the monographs and articles of Professor Dreinach, in fine bindings. Some possessions are stored in cupboards and drawers, and there are what might be called sacramental rites in fetching them out, unwrapping, explaining, handling, laying whatever it might be to rest again in tissue-paper and cotton-wool. Specially preserved treasures include the Czar's silver cigarette box, and the red morocco box containing the patent of nobility from the Kaiser.

When Henriette says that she believes in fate, she really means the abiding presence of her father. The spirit of Baron Gustav occupies Perry's Ridge, and the little house can hardly contain something so nearly occult within its neat walls. His eyes were incredibly powerful, Henriette says, to look into them was like looking into eternity. What can my mother have made of such a dynamic man ? A force of nature. But then she died young, like Rudi, and like Jules – they all died before their time.

'Nowadays they'd only have to give Rudi anti-biotics and he'd be all right. Blood-poisoning, I ask you.'

Rex says, 'No good crying over spilt milk. Go on, tell The Boy everything, he ought to know his family history, you can see how he's aching to hear it.'

After the row and the parting, Jules wrote letters. From Sagodvar. The letters are always locked in a safe place.

'When can I see them ?'

'As soon as you're old enough to understand.'

'And when will that be ?'

Miss Butley does lunch, and prepares dishes for supper. Every day she walks from the village with a string shopping bag in her hand, but it is always inexplicably empty, she seems to bring it just in case. In the house she has remained practically invisible and inaudible, except for 'Yes madam' and 'Yes, Mr Rex', often followed by a clearing of the throat so shy that it twists into a suppressed cough. Bandy-legged, her hair pulled back in a bun, she is a living apology for taking up any space at all. Not even Henriette could have raised her voice to Miss Butley. Actually the two of them have stayed on the most level terms. The kitchen has brought them together. At Pernsdorf and Sagodvar, Henriette hardly knew where the servants' quarters were.

Gardening occupied Rex in the afternoon. In my ignorance, he appeared to be an expert, planting out herbaceous borders, taking cuttings, fussing about tulip bulbs in the shed, ordering from catalogues. The compost heap was his hobby. Whatever flowers were in season were cut and arranged by him in vases for the house. Heavy work, such as digging or mowing the lawns, was done by Mr Whalton. When he could be persuaded to work, Mr Whalton never stopped. From my bedroom I could hear him hard at it with a wheelbarrow or a spade up to the moment when the light finally faded on the longest summer days. Rex might be out with him, weeding or pruning. Nobody was allowed to touch his secateurs or his leather gloves.

The Whaltons lived in a cottage visible from Perry's Ridge. To walk there through the trees was to cross a frontier into drama and chaos. In spite of Mr Whalton's skills, his own garden was almost derelict, with a cracked basin half-buried in it, and scraps of rusted saucepans and bicycles amid blackcurrants whose netting had long since vanished. A wild animal reek filled the cottage. Mrs Whalton wore the same woolly sweater and skirt, and flimsy pink slippers indoors and out. Right into the height of summer, she complained about the cold and liked to position herself close to the coal-burning range, in an arm-chair whose seat was collapsing. Lack of engagement reached the point of vacancy when it came to bringing up her four daughters. Susie, the eldest, was obliged to do everything for the other three. I admired Susie's looks, her hazel eyes, the quickness with which she moved. She was sporty. There came a day when Susie climbed on a fence, slipped, and gashed high up on her thigh. The wound at first opened white, then blood began to spring deep within it, gathering and running down her leg. We screamed as we raced to the cottage. Mrs Whalton seemed to take for ever before finding a cloth to soak in water and tie round the gash. In the end, stitches were required. For a special favour, Susie afterwards pulled aside her clothes for anyone who wanted to see the ridged and discoloured scar, and run a finger over it. Whenever the muddle of her parents boiled over into outright crisis, it was Susie who came over to ask Henriette, 'May we borrow some bread and milk?' In return Mr Whalton made me a rabbit-hutch, which took him a year. The carpentry looked exquisite.

Playing, we children often caught sight of Rex slipping out of the back of the house, into the wood and on down to the village. He took a silver-handled stick. Ahead of him, Robbie the fat labrador crossed and recrossed the path between the trees until both were lost.

In early years at Perry's Ridge, so I am told, a woman by the name of Denny looked after me. There was also someone called Margaret. My recollection is of Henriette, alone in the house, occupied with me; on her knees at the edge of the bath while she soaps me slippery all over; pulling me into flannel pyjamas and a dressing-gown with a tasselled cord; heating up a drink with a spoonful of malt in it, last thing at night, before climbing the steep stairs to the attic.

A nightmare used to pursue me. I was in my room, telling myself that I was really awake, not dreaming at all. Closing around me were banks of flowers. I must be awake, because their scent was so strong, I was almost drugged by it. Go on, smell them, a voice was urging, deeper than Rex's but with his inflections so that I was unable to decide if it really was him talking to me. Too late, I perceived that the flowers were closing in on me, that they were not flowers at all but something unknown and living, the petals were really claws, I was being slashed and razored, my blood was transfused and what had been flowers were revealed red with it, fleshy. Forcing myself to stand up and look out of the dormer window across the valley, I could check if I was safely awake only by placing a hand on my beating heart. Below, Rex and Mr Whalton might be tidying up in the dusk, smoking a last cigarette.

The closest friends of Rex and Henriette were the Engle-hearts, who lived in a grand stone house on the far side of the village. They had left Germany in 1933. Mr Engleheart had been a consulting engineer, had travelled over much of the world, and was still often away. Among his international acquaintances were Arab and African leaders – in 1955 he was an advisor over the Aswan Dam. Further away lived Mrs Esterbrook who was Viennese, which somehow entitled her to claims upon Henriette. A district nurse, she drove a small Morris, and found some pretext or other to pass by Perry's Ridge. She dyed her hair the colour of marmalade and looked as if she put make-up on without benefit of a mirror, smearing it thick here and there. Unlike the Englehearts, she invited me to tea and gave me presents. 'Esterbrook is not Esterhazy,' Henriette said, to convey that in former days the ladies would not have known one another. Now they combined to meet in one house or another, to play bridge and canasta, six-pack bezique and cribbage. Rex and Mr Engleheart also compared notes about cross-words.

On Sundays Henriette and Rex attended morning service in the parish church. The choir wore blue surplices and frilly collars. Mrs Esterbrook's voice was that much louder than anyone else's, as though to show that she knew what a proper soprano could do. We always sat in the same pew, the third from the front, embarrassingly close to the pulpit when it was time for the sermon. On the war memorial on the wall are seventeen names in alphabetical order from Private Richard Attrill of the West Kent Regiment to Lieutenant William

Bosworth Younger of the Royal Engineers. I could recite the whole inscription. Outside the porch, after the service, we greeted the vicar, Miss Butley, everyone, but somehow as the others drifted away, Henriette, Rex, Mrs Esterbrook and the Englehearts, if they were there, were left standing in the churchyard, in their voices the grate and pitch of accents and idioms that none of them except Rex had mastered properly. German was never spoken, although it was the mother tongue of every one of them, again excepting Rex, of course.

•*Thirty One*•

The Humber was a pre-war model, in vintage green with ribbed upholstery a deeper but matching colour. More than sedate, it was stately. At the wheel Rex slowed down to let everyone else pass, a process more like steering than driving, and for some reason known as 'letting the crate have her head.' Such extreme caution on the road was itself a danger. Perhaps – I wonder now – he held no licence.

Expeditions to London were constantly planned, but rarely occurred. 'The Boy's got to be properly dressed,' he would say. 'We'll have to use the rest of the coupons on that scarecrow, it can't be helped. We'll take in a show too.' Or he had friends to meet, a lawyer, the dentist, the man from the claim's department of the Foreign Office, tailors.

'I can't afford it.'

Henriette's veto came in that form.

'The Boy needs it, people will be laughing at him' – though who these people might be was not spelled out. His skill lay in convincing her that what really she had wanted to do all along was actually conferring a favour on us.

I must have been about eight or nine at the time of this particular clothes' buying. The Humber was parked in a garage underground. Then we caught taxis. In one department store after another, Rex made a song and dance about The Boy needs this, The Boy needs that. So many ration points here, so many there – I can hear the satisfactory snip of scissors clipping them out.

Lunch was in a hotel. Its hall was a vista of marble. During the war Henriette and Rex had been habitual guests, and were greeted by the doorman and the concierge. Ever since, for me a treat has had something to do with food prepared beside the table in a dining-room, with *hors d'oeuvres* on a trolley, freshly starched linen and folded napkins. Meals at Perry's Ridge were not like this. I noticed how Henriette opened her handbag, counted out notes, and then bending down in her chair she passed this money to Rex in a gesture only clumsily covered by the table-cloth. It was then he who paid the bill, he who joked with the headwaiter.

'To business,' Rex said. It was arranged that we should meet again in the evening, and meanwhile Henriette took me to the cinema. Back in the hall of the hotel, we began to wait for Rex. I had a book to read. Time passed. Henriette removed her watch and held it in her hand. Her face began to alter until it expressed nothing but active rage. Since that time, I have discovered a great deal more about this impressive temper. She cannot help herself, it is conditioned, the consequence of her privileged upbringing, and therefore to be considered an integral part of Baron Gustav's legacy. Colour drains out of the cheeks, the flesh appears to become as hard as plaster, a sort of death-mask descends. The whole head is simplified into a square, at the centre of which are the eyes, ringed black like targets. She stares but seems not to be focusing. As though the blood system were erupting and there were inner seismic disturbances, she quakes. She becomes much too angry to explain herself.

Hours after the agreed time and long after I was supposed to be in bed, Rex arrived. Some kind of scuffle took place on the pavement. The doorman was supporting him, had an arm round his waist, half-dragged him over to the reception desk. A certain aplomb kept him upright there, but his feet began to slither and give way, and he folded down on his knees. People were looking at the spectacle. I assumed that he was ill, and was amazed that Henriette could stay where she was, so hostile and implacable. The doorman and the lift-boy hauled Rex up, and helped him to the lift. A long time seemed to pass before Henriette was ready to walk over to the receptionist. I heard her saying, 'And a separate room for my grandson.'

I understood that what was happening was no novelty, had its routine. This was not illness, then, special action was not required. The room into which I was shown had two beds. It was an adventure to be there without pyjamas, unable to brush my teeth. The day's shopping lay about in bulky parcels. Sandwiches were brought in, and I was allowed to eat them in bed.

'What's wrong? I asked.

'It's from the war. It can't be helped, so we have to be careful, but it doesn't last long, you'll see how quickly he recovers.'

The colour returning to her face was all wrong; the lips were stretched thin and mauve, and in contrast to the eyes and the deep circles in which they were set, her hair looked quite white.

Next day Rex drove the Humber as usual, but on the way home we sat in silence, in the tail-end of the storm of Henriette's temper.

It was Susie who explained the thing to me.

'Where do you think they go, then, him and me dad through the woods? Don't be daft. Down to the Rose and Crown. You watch it. When they're like that, they wallop you.'

But that Rex never did.

·*Thirty Two*·

Every few months the postman used to deliver packages wrapped in a shiny brown paper, with astonishing stamps and stickers on it. The packages were addressed to me, I was fetched in order to undo them, pulling out tins of pineapple and peaches, jars of cooking fat, crumbled cookies. Also clothes, including shoes several sizes too large, and a winter sweater that hung off my shoulders. The packages came from Chicago and the sender was Oscar Webber, or so it said on the wrapping paper.

'I receive letters from our orphans all over the world,' Henriette told me, 'but none of them are so faithful as Oscar Webber.'

Our orphans. This was a phrase, perhaps an item, like Pernsdorf or Sagodvar or the candlesticks of the noble savages, which belonged to quite another dimension. I slipped into it as into a fairy-story. But the packages from Chicago proved the reality.

Oscar Webber turned out to be squat and over-weight, not the least like the prince of the packages that I had visualised. His head was thrust forward on his shoulders. What hair he had was untidy, and he seems never quite to have completed the morning's shave. To this day, Oscar speaks a kind of German-American to which justice cannot be done; Emigranto, he calls it. He looks bothered, as if he cannot find time for all the things he would like to be doing. It is a nervous habit of his to be simultaneously talking and grabbing at your arm or elbow.

'I came over on the *Queen Mary*,' said Oscar Webber, 'just for a sight of this kid.'

Perhaps he had sent me the outsize shoes and sweater

because he cannot help imagining people and things larger than life. One of his presents was a tie with a woman painted on it, who seemed to be clothed until held up to the light when she turned quite phosphorescent and naked. He also brought boxes of American sweets, the kind with a hole in them, unknown in England at the time.

'You have no idea what it means to me to be able to do something for the family, it was *the* family of Vienna,' he says. 'The Waisenhaus gave us everything, it is an honour, a privilege, to be able to render a little bit back. Every one of us would do the same. In the States we have formed an association, Sprinzak in San Diego, the New Jersey people with Schattner. You'll meet them one day, you'll stay with us. Helga will look after you, and my two boys, we've made good over there, that's where the future is.'

Though there was a guest room, he preferred to stay at the Rose and Crown, saying, 'I couldn't presume to accept the gracious lady's hospitality.'

My first bicycle was a present from Oscar. Out on the road he ran behind me, his hand on the bicycle to keep it steady while I wobbled and pedalled. As he sweated, his hair stuck to his scalp like string.

'Your father was a very fine young man,' he said. 'Don't you ever forget it, it's why you bear his name. We'd be about the same age. I was in the Waisenhaus when he sat himself before the piano and played it, we'd had no warning. Incredible. It was magnificent. A genius, like Baron Gustav, in a different line of country but a genius all the same. They can kill the flesh but not the spirit, and don't you ever forget that either.'

Unlike Oscar Webber, Marietta Revertella stayed in the house, and for long periods too. Her husband, Pier-Luigi Carrassi, a man from her own background, was making a career for himself in the Italian Communist Party. The marriage was not a success; she was already using her maiden name. When the husband insisted that she sell the Sargent portrait of her mother, she hoped that Henriette would buy it. I can remember Henriette saying, 'Poor Mimi, I would have to rebuild the whole place to fit her in.'

Rex liked Marietta. She made him laugh. She talks faultless English and certainly she brought the outside world into Perry's Ridge during those years of post-war austerity. In spite of her air of suffering nobly endured, Marietta was not so poor that she had to dispense with the New Look and Dior.

Whether or not she really is the sister of Henriette, on the wrong side of the blanket, will never be established. Both of them encourage the notion because even at their age they seem to want to humanise their parents.

'Toni and I used to stand in front of the mirror so that we could see ourselves clearly, front and back and in profile. Who did we look like most?' Marietta will say. 'Toni had my father's figure. True. I'm more down to earth like Baron Gustav, I'd be as fat if I let myself eat what I want. Mimi took the secret with her to the grave. We searched and searched, but found no evidence.'

'Mimi was a darling,' Henriette says. 'Ferdy was such a gentleman too, he never showed any jealousy. He couldn't have accepted Concordia money if he thought his children were Gustav's.'

'Of course he could,' Rex says. 'Someone has to pay the bills.'

It is summer. The borders are a mass of reds and blues. Out on the lawn which Mr Whalton has mowed in symmetrical stripes, croquet hoops have been set up. Rex is teaching Marietta the game. 'Put your legs apart like a good girl,' he says, 'Hoick up that pretty skirt and swing the mallet straight, go on, biff it.'

We sit in deck-chairs. For tea, vanilla biscuits are served on a plate. Marietta turns to me.

'I'm pretty well the last person to have seen your father alive. I adored him. We would have done anything for him, I want you to know that. Toni and I had leave, we went to Sagodvar. Toni had been a fascist, he supported Hitler in the beginning but he'd come to realise his mistake, he regretted it. He and Jules were like brothers, Toni felt responsible ever since we'd all gone up in an aeroplane as children, and the plane dived and Jules hit his head. We children thought it was

152

all our fault, but of course it was just an accident. Jules was in his own world, he didn't seem to take it in about concentration camps.'

'What is a concentration camp?'

Rex stands behind her chair, places his hands on her shoulders.

'Why does everyone have to talk to The Boy about those things? Leave him alone. Time for more croquet too.'

·Thirty Three·

High Hampton is still approached through banks of rhodo-dendrons. Abruptly the house appears, its stonework cold and grey, but with a view of the playing-fields beyond. Henriette and Rex escorted me there. 'Cheer up,' Rex was saying, 'What we used to sing in rather similar circumstances was a song with the words, "We don't want to lose you but we think you ought to go."'

'The dump,' Rex says. 'Rather jolly, and I loved it here till my Henny called me to higher things.'

In my day the school belonged to the Freans, who had bought it from the Kingdoms. Hechter J. is painted in capitals on a board in the main passageway and Mr Frean shows it to us. Another generation, he says: where I am concerned, he has been making up instant tradition.

Sniffing the air like a terrier, Rex gives a conducted tour. His study, once upon a time; the music-room, recalling arrangements he used to make for Jules to play the piano with Mrs Stokes; bathrooms, quite unchanged, down to the tiling and the duck-boards; squashed-fly biscuits still to eat, and treacle pudding. Only the air-raid shelter is new, and already useless. There is a walk to be done to the park wall, where Jules and Immington and Stavrakis had done battle famously with the gang of village boys. Things have changed, village boys have vanished and their former homes have been smartened up for commuters.

'That's the window I had to pay for, the other parents refused.'

Henriette points with her umbrella. However many Sundays we traipsed off to church, I never could spot which of the windows had been repaired.

154

'The great thing is never to let yourself be bullied. I'm not paying for any more damages.'

'One look at Killer-eyes here, and bullies would run for their lives.'

Of course there was no bullying at High Hampton. Far from it. The terms passed in dizzying good-will and endeavour. Freudians, Quakers, trained in social work and education theories, the Freans and their staff were one and all quick on to anything unseemly, as buzzards on a mouse.

A school like that, with a high moral and pacifist line, has a library which has been carefully pre-selected for right-thinking. It was there, in the glass-fronted book-case, that the key to the past lay waiting to be discovered. A large book bound in cloth had no lettering on the spine or on its cover, which was mysterious, leaving it untitled. To open it was an unforgettable shock. Several hundred photographs illustrated exactly what concentration camps had been. So this was what had happened, this was what was not spoken about at Perry's Ridge. Whenever possible, I used to go and secrete myself in a corner of the reading-room to absorb that book and its contents. The paper was rather coarse, I had the faded but slightly sickly smell of it under my nostrils. The duty-master spotted me, became suspicious, said that the book was for reference purposes only, and that I had looked at it quite long enough. So when the coast was clear, I stole it, hid it, and took it home and have it still.

In dreams, flowers no longer smother me and slash my cheeks to ribbons. I move in that Book of the Dead. I am on a train. No doors, no windows. The others are fighting for space in which to stand, for air to breathe, but around me seems to be space and light. I squat on the wooden floor as the train rocks in a journey through the night. Next to me is an old man, his legs stretched out. He has a beard, a hat, boots, an overcoat, and he fusses over a suitcase. Protectively he wants to explain, thankfully I can trust him. He speaks, I listen, I tell myself that I must listen and understand. He knows where to find Jules and Litzi, he picks up the suitcase, a passage opens for him among the other people, and he is at once lost among them. If they were there, I would know – God help me, I have the book, I turn it upside down to stare at the photographs from every angle for faces I might recognise.

Thirty Four

We are on the sofas in the drawing-room at Perry's Ridge. The bars of the electric heater are all switched on. It is the week after Christmas and in that year I must have been fourteen. We are sated with food. It is also a moment, the only moment, when Henriette allows bottles to be unlocked in the house. Rex has mixed a cocktail before lunch, and he keeps the wine on the table. You do not have to offer Henriette a penny for her thoughts. Her nose sticks up in the air. Only the presence of Mrs Esterbrook prevents her swooping on the drink.

Mrs Esterbrook has to leave early. She wants to be home before the day draws in. A marvellous winter day, with a vaporous sky, the sun hanging like a copper medal but unable to draw the frost off the ground.

'Let's make an expedition,' Rex says. He is all enthusiasm. Twenty minutes off is a National Trust house, with a famous park.

'Before it's dark, come on you lazy lot.'

Rex struggles into his camel-hair coat, claps his hands. Mrs Esterbrook drives one way, we another, in the magic radiance of the afternoon. Much of the country-side has the gleam of this cold spell. Frost on the branches of the trees, along the line of hedges. Smoke drifts up out of chimneys into the wind-less air. The gates of the National Trust house are open. Nobody is about, and perhaps we are trespassing. The drive leads up to a classical facade, with a turning down to the lake. Rex pulls up, and to stay warm, Henriette decides to remain in the Humber. Robbie the dog, shaking himself, circles back to the car. The whole lake is frozen over, dazzling as crystal. Around it, reeds edge up black and sharp, in frosty clumps.

'We couldn't be funking it, could we?'

Before I can answer, Rex has slipped his arm through mine, and we are away on ice which at that point has been corrugated by the wind.

I am supporting a deadweight as he leans on me. The camel-hair coat is like padding against my anorak. The tongue of its belt hangs down. On his head is a Russian-style cap in some black fur.

The ice might not bear us. Now and again, reports go off underfoot like gun-shots, and zig-zag cracks race inches deep through the ice, though without parting it. Behind us, Robbie skulks unhappily. In the middle of the lake, the surface has frozen choppily and unevenly, Rex slides forward in his galoshes as though on skates. I cannot wriggle out of his hold, and there is no turning back.

A boathouse stands on the far shore, at the end of a wooden jetty, with open access for a rowing-boat. The jetty leads to an interior platform. In the corner of this shelter, Rex removes his gloves and in the half-dark the signet-ring and the blue enamel or opaline ring seem to flash on his hands. The black fur hat falls on to the platform. He scuffs at the belt of his coat, and is grabbing me, pulling at me. A spider's web of broken little veins radiates from the nose outwards and upwards at the top of his cheeks, towards the blue eyes. His mouth takes on the shape of a small slack bag, his breath smells of drink. The bristly face rasps against mine as I dodge, my shout is stifled in his scarf and flapping coat, and I lash out to break the bony grip on my shoulders.

Henriette is standing just outside the boat-house. The sun has faded into damson-dusk twilight, the temperature is dropping to several degrees below freezing. No movement, no sound from that dumpy figure. I have no means of knowing what she saw nor what she guessed, as I run away and Rex stoops to recover his fur cap.

•*Thirty Five*•

Dicky is an old family friend, they said, who wants to take an interest in you, like an uncle. He'll offer you cakes and a cup of tea, you'll have the chance for a good talk, you might be taken to the theatre or the opera.

Dicky Harwood was the sort of man Rex collected, without explanation of how they had met, or at what point in the past. The man lived alone in north London, and Mr Frean accompanied me from High Hampton on my first visit. His task was to impress on me the right train, the right bus, how to recognise the detached red-brick villa on its tree-lined street. Afterwards I was to go every Wednesday in term-time, missing the sports afternoon, which was a pity as I liked football. Every week Mr Frean advanced me the money for the trip, and used to allow me to keep any spare coins as extra pocket-money.

The room in which we sat had windows with leaded panes. The lights were always on. It seemed bleak and uncomfortable, even for a bachelor. We faced one another in arm-chairs, but I had no idea how to make conversation to this lonely and uncommunicative stranger. Over-dressed in a pinstripe suit, he wore the same bow-tie, and smoked a pipe which he knocked out a good deal of the time, like a man signalling in morse code. That tapping drove everything of interest out of my mind, leaving it to register how bald the man was, and how boring. There was never any question of the theatre or opera. At the end of the hour, the air had become grey and stale ; at last I was free to race down the path out into the street, and then on to the bus-stop. Lucky you, the other boys at High Hampton said.

The meaning of the Wednesday sessions was clarified in the

holidays, quite by accident. Behind the backs of Henriette and Rex, I used often to make rather a nuisance of myself to Freda Butley, way-laying her as she did the house-work and in general distracting the poor woman. While doing so, I happened to catch sight in Rex's room of several sheets of writing-paper with a name and address in bold lettering at the top : Dr Richard Harwood. The man was a doctor? Then my eye caught references to me.

There could be no doubt, the doctor wrote, that he was confronting a seriously disturbed child. Weighty language was thrown about concerning neurosis and classic syndromes and obsessions. What appeared to be ingratitude on my part for their kindness in bringing me up was primarily an expression of longing for the parents I had never known, and that had to be overlooked. Every orphan fantasised about his parents, and my fantasies had an emotional stranglehold on me. The case was complicated because I resented Henriette's money, and Rex's access to it; I felt that the entire family legacy came to me, should already by rights be mine. There was a consoling aspect to it, in that orphans normally mistake money for security – had not Baron Gustav himself been a case in point ? Perhaps if he was to practise a course of several years of therapy, he might straighten out a thoroughly nasty child.

Snoopers, according to convention, rarely learn anything to their advantage. Once Freda Butley was out of the way, I returned to read the report more slowly. Until then, I had not realised how I feared and hated Rex. My heart was set racing. Here was a declaration of war. Him or me. Of course I had been brought up aware of the circumstances of his entry into the family. In the orthodox version, he had perceptively realised what a threat the Nazis were, had devised the means of saving part of Henriette's fortune, and provided her with English nationality and a refuge. Jules, it had been implied, had short-sightedly picked a quarrel with him, and if he had not been too proud to make it up might still have been alive. Holding Dr Richard Harwood's sheets of paper in my hand, I had quite different insights. Facts fell into place – no doubt that would have happened anyhow in due course. A drunk. A homosexual. A parasite. As devious as he was unscrupulous. One or other of us would have to go. Fantasies, indeed. I imagined myself unmasking him, freeing a grateful Henriette, watching him walk empty-handed from the house, restoring natural justice.

Smail-Turner : the double-barrelled sound of it had always been bogus. Why had he no relations ? I bicycled five or six miles to the nearest post-office containing every telephone directory. Checking through them, I found nobody of that name anywhere in the country.

Oundle was reputed to have featured in Rex's past. Also the Durham Light Infantry. So I wrote to the public school and to the regiment to inquire for details. Those were anxious moments while I waited for answers which did not arrive, while the holidays ebbed away. The postman was a friend, but his round was irregular and I had to intercept him before he reached the house. Both letters arrived on the same morning, with hardly any time to spare. Neither at Oundle nor in the Durham Light Infantry could they help me, they regretted to say ; the records showed nobody of that name.

A burst of pity for Henriette seized me. Obviously Rex's foremost victim, she needed affection. 'What's the matter with you?' she asked, when I said that I did not want to return to school but would stay with her. The letters were safe under my vest, I could put a hand to them and feel the underlying crackle, but it was impossible to pull them out and reveal their contents. Hopeless. I had no idea how to expose Rex, I did not dare do it.

In the course of the first Wednesday session with Dr Harwood during the new term, political calculations were abandoned.

'You're a doctor,' I blurted out, 'a psychiatrist.'

'Not exactly, but that kind of thing.'

I should have been told. It was the moral equivalent of spying on me. Had I really been in control of the situation, I would have confronted Dr Harwood with the two letters I was cherishing ; that would have been successful retaliation.

He must have found confirmation for his theories about how disturbed and unpleasant a child I was because I simply fled from him, in such a hurry that I did not shut the front door after me and he came out shouting but I was already far away, and sprinting. The sensation of being free to wander at will into London shops stays with me today as some sort of voluptuous peak.

Mr Frean met me at the station. I was treated as though playing truant, when the opposite was the case, and I was obeying the time-table.

Henriette and Rex came down. They took me to lunch in the country hotel usually frequented by visiting parents.

'Poor Dicky's dreadfully hurt, he thought you were getting on so fine with him.'

'We couldn't cope with teenage rebellion,' Henriette said. 'We're too old for that kind of thing. Not after all we've done for you. We didn't take that into account.'

'The fact is', I replied to Rex, 'that I told him how you call me Killer-eyes and he became frightfully excited, and wanted to know lots more which I think it right to be telling him.'

This was the one and only occasion when I saw Rex put out, distinctly cross, but it closed the matter of psycho-analysis.

No child is able to get the measure of an adult's concern for him. Within a few weeks I was once again summoned to Mr Frean's rooms. As I knocked and entered, there was Stavrakis, explaining to Mr Frean the loyalties of Old Boys like himself. Until that moment he had played a lesser part in my life than Oscar Webber or Marietta, the kind of guest at Perry's Ridge who arrived already apologising that he would have to leave at once.

'It's engraved on every English boy's heart that school is the happiest time of his life,' Stavrakis said in front of a smiling Mr Frean. The moment we were alone, he put the record straight by adding, 'I hope you aren't an English boy. As a matter of fact, this was and is and always will be a dump, they must have been crazy to send you here. I expect you're top of your form the way we were, because the rest are so thick.'

He drives his sports car flat out, with fines for speeding in half a dozen countries, the pieces of paper are crammed under the dashboard. Swiss number plates, which cause less trouble everywhere, he says. Nor are country hotels good enough for him when it comes to taking out a boy from school.

'Jules was my closest friend, I want you to know that I'd do anything for you. I'm the last left of our lot, Immington was in the American navy, his destroyer was sunk in the Pacific.'

As though he were still a schoolboy, nobody seems to call Stavrakis by his first name of Nikos, and he himself refuses to admit to growing older. He is black-eyed and black-haired, though with grey in it. His skin is lightly flecked, which gives him a hard look, like weathered stone. He can still wear the suits he had as a twenty-year-old, and perhaps he would if he were not so conscious of his appearance : hand-made shirts and shoes, ties from Rome and Paris. He sports cuff-links in chunks of gold large enough to be investments, and he was the first person I ever noticed to have an expandable strap, also gold, on his wrist-watch. As if to hurry himself along to the next appointment, he has a way of shaking that watch and strap. Surplus vitality in all he does. His flat is in Paris, where he operates as European manager of one of the giant car manufacturers in Detroit. The lady whom he refers to as 'the mother of my children' lives in Athens, and Stavrakis seems to be a walking airline schedule. Into his English comes the throb of a slight American accent.

On impulse I told Stavrakis how Rex nicknamed me Killer-eyes, how its meaning became clear when he had forced me across the frozen lake, and had grabbed at me in the boat-house although I was reasonably sure that Henriette had been within sight.

'Maybe she has a kick out of it,' he said. 'She's odd herself, or why else should she marry a homosexual? And not just one, but two.'

When I showed him the two letters, he roared with laughter. 'Listening to you,' he said, 'I have the impression that time has stood still. For God's sake, Jules used to have identical conversations by the hour. I've spent a lifetime wondering what's to be done about Rex, how to get him off our backs. Here goes another generation.'

His wallet was crocodile-skin, its corners tipped with gold, and from behind the photographs in it he pulled out a hundred dollar note.

'Indispensable for the girls,' he said. 'You'll know when to use it. How are you with the girls?'

At that moment my voice was breaking, more or less; certainly I had not started to shave.

'Leave it to me,' Stavrakis said.

When that summer term came to an end and I left High Hampton, I did not realise that I should never see the place again. Slowly, but with great good humour, Rex and Henriette revealed the arrangements that had been made. A fresh start. The plan was that I should accept the invitation of Oscar Webber and stay with him in America, go to school there for at least a term, perhaps a year or even longer if it was a success. Stavrakis had business to do, we could fly together.

Rex was ill that holiday, with a recurrence of the trouble on his lungs. Dr Clarke ordered him to stop smoking. 'This is not a house in which I can expect much cooperation,' Dr Clarke said. But Rex stayed in bed. Trays were carried up by all of us, including Mrs Esterbrook who enjoyed crisis. The labrador lay across his feet.

'Sit on the bed,' he said to me. 'There's plenty of room for you and Robbie, go on.'

He was in a dressing-gown, and a silk scarf was wrapped around his throat. Because he had become thinner, he appeared to have aged, his hair to be whiter, but he had not lost that easy manner of his.

'Now you're going out into the great wide world, you won't find it quite the awful place you think it is. Actually there's lots of fun to be had. Try it, you'll see. Open up, don't be such a prig.'

He hesitated. I could see that something was on his mind.

'Though I say it as shouldn't, I did a lot for Jules. I'd have liked to have helped you too, but you wouldn't have it, Boy, now would you? Oh, go on.'

The moment of confession, if that was what it had been, passed into silence and stalemate.

'All together in the floral dance,' he sang as he waved me out.

·Thirty Six·

Oscar and Helga Webber live in a Chicago suburb. Until I saw the district, I had not appreciated what a success they had made of their lives. Lawns are emerald there, the swimming pools wide and deep. Even the side-walks are swept as tidily as carpets. In summer the pool house is open, in winter the storm-windows are hung up. Oscar's attitude is, Let's have everything that money can buy, what else is the stuff for except to secure everyday life? Under the extravagance is a sense that the system which has thrown up such material wealth might just as unexpectedly take it all back. Helga especially has worries on that score, she does not like anyone to help her in the house, liking to be sure that she can do it on her own; she also attends evening classes in sociology with the idea that one day she is going to be into social work, at the receiving or the giving end, according to how the mood takes her. They keep a Jewish home, Oscar says Kiddush on sabbath, they celebrate the High Holidays, they fast on Yom Kippur, they seem to regret that they are not more orthodox than they are, for the sake of their sons, Gus and Igi, other-wise Gustav and Ignacz.

'Every day I give thanks,' Oscar says, and he means it. 'We have all been so lucky.'

Work at it, he has always urged me, learn German, write a book about your family, tell everyone about Gustav Ellingen. Now there was a man. To bring back millions in gold when the war was lost, in order to save his factories. What an example. A good Jew, a great man. Tell them about Henriette, and Jules.

Early in the morning before the freeway chokes up, Oscar leaves for the office down-town. Something is wrong with his

166

vision, he says, so he leaves the driving to Gus, and by now he seems to have handed over much of the business to him as well. A hardware store was the beginning of their fortune. Retailing, according to Oscar, is the best way to learn about humanity, and he has built up a chain of stores. Bigger money has been made through developing shopping centres and plazas. His friends and associates are much like him. I have met Schattner and the New Jersey crowd, and Sprinzak from San Diego. Learn German, they insist in their turn, tell the truth, speak up for the dead.

'Your father could hardly reach the key-board, he was a shrimp. We had no warning that he'd play, he would have been another Horovitz, another Rubinstein.'

Gus and Igi had been to High School before me, they acted as guides to the America of ball-games, french fries, deep-necking girls, votes for the Classmate Most Likely to Succeed. From the start Gus has wanted me to join him in the family business. Igi recommends law-school, through which he is putting himself.

'The Frau Baronin will be lonely, she'll miss you,' Oscar repeats. 'You must fly home, it isn't nice.'

Some reason always cropped up for staying put. Once we drove, all five of us, to friends in Vancouver. In Kansas, Oscar had a project. 'Stay,' Helga says. 'One more man about the house, it's a pleasure.'

The call from Henriette with the news that Rex was seriously ill seemed unbelievable. A thousand times before, I had heard descriptions of his bad health, I thought it self-indulgence or make-believe, part of the fiction about serving with the Durham Light Infantry. This latest infection of the lungs sounded like all the others. But I was wrong.

Henriette was alone with him when he died. A letter from solicitors had the information that Rex had made me his heir. 'His happiness and welfare has been such a concern', in the words of the short will, 'that I bequeath to the young Julius Hechter, grandson of my beloved wife, everything that I possess at the time of my demise.'

This actually meant, as I discovered at Perry's Ridge, the

clothes in his cupboard, his silver-handled walking stick, and the two rings he had always worn. These latter I returned to Henriette.

·*Thirty Seven*·

Sagodvar writing-paper had been blue, and its letter-head with the address and telephone number, Zalaszentistvan One, was engraved in red. The envelopes were lined, and on them were stamps in maroon and emerald green, with the head and shoulders of Admiral Horthy. Those letters posted after the start of the war had been slit open down one side, and resealed with white tape by a censor identified only by a printed number in four or sometimes five figures. Jules's handwriting looked unhurried, elegantly formed.

12 October 1938.

Schatz! You are so much in my thoughts. This house has never looked more beautiful. The woods have the spectacular Indian summer colours which you so enjoy. Sometimes I wake up and think, oh good, we can all make an expedition or go sight-seeing, and then reality comes flooding in. And perhaps it is for the best that you are where you are. Your next step surely ought to be to move out of the flat, it must be far too cramping. Don't you really prefer the country? Some of the villages around High Hampton are as pretty as could be, and full of unexpected people too. I write this no longer out of a wish to make good blood between us all but as a simple matter of common-sense.

The *Abkommen* (Munich Agreement) is welcomed, most people believe that the peace will be preserved now, and that in any case whatever the Czechs get they richly deserve. The newspapers are rather fierce. It is a temptation, fatal perhaps, to withdraw from the world, to indulge in what gives pleasure, to luxuriate here. I've been working on the *polonaises*, hence the Chopin split-personality. Endre Schuster has been here, he proposes that we go to Turkey. Geza shot some partridges with me, *il est toujours tellement bon garçon*, I spent a happy weekend afterwards at Felsöjattö.

Professor Reischl came for the night, and Kathi and Palla, Irma Grunberger and your old love, the Rittmeister. Production records are being beaten in the harvesting, the Egyedys are fine and send a warm *Küss die Hand an die Herrschaften*. In the village there is great excitement over an unusual number of pregnancies, at least a dozen, an epidemic. Some say that the ladies have discovered a special prescription, but those who know better declare that the prescription is actually Dr F. himself.

23 November 1938.

In haste, because we have a man here to buy pigs, and he will post the letter on his way through Gyor. There is a chance that I may visit Quappi, the Verweys live in Groeningen, and if I get there I will hop on over across the Channel. The difficulty is that I may have no right to re-enter this country, my permit is temporary, conditional, and they all shake their heads over it. We shall have to see.

15 April 1939.

Your last letter cheers me up no end every time I read it. I miss you dreadfully and see no solution to that. Wonderful to hear that you have found a place in the country within easy reach of London. I very well remember motoring with you and Papa through Sussex, and how we enjoyed the Downs and stopped to look at the incredible collection of pictures at Petworth. That sort of thing, and of course scones and muffins and gentleman's relish is *ce qui fait la force de l'Angleterre*. Perry's Ridge has a good strong ring about it. You and Rex will enjoy making the garden. An English garden, please, with lots of red, white and blue flowers in Union Jack rows.

Across the frontier the picture is dreadful. Poor Margulies, I can hardly believe that the poor man has been dead a year already, their despair affects me as if it was yesterday. Rumour reaches us that the factory and the house are cared for but one hardly knows what to believe and nobody dares put much on paper. Suffering done by Austrians and Czechs gives quiet satisfaction here, sometimes not even quiet but loud. I have seen Moritz Sobollia, the old Schaffgotsch who is under the impression that the Kaiser Franz Josef is still alive in the Hofburg, and Toni and Marietta write with plans. We see eye to eye, especially on *il gran signior*. What an absolute ape.

9 December 1939.

Now that things have turned out the way they have, I feel more of a fool than ever. An idiot pure and simple. Rex was clear-sighted about what had to be done, the facts have proved it, it's far too late in the day to be bothered with flattery. Practically the only consolation is that the two of you are safe, settling in Perry's Ridge. What will happen next, you must know better than me. Sleeping Beauty occupies our stage. Troubles with passport and resident's permit and papers have been resolved for the time being, thanks to Geza. Without him, I don't know what I would have done. The captain of the gendarmerie in Gyor turns out to be a friend to us. We all had lunch, and I am in order for another twelve months. All the man wants in return is to walk up the partridges. In a year, things ought to be clearer. The Budapest lawyers are totally useless and a waste of time, but we didn't need a war to learn that.

Irma has been dreadfully ill and wants to convalesce here. Old Frau Schuster died, Endre did not return for the funeral, he's in Turkey and he's staying there.

16 January 1940.

Your sweet birthday letter reached me eight weeks late. Like Verlaine, or is it Rimbaud, you might well ask, *oh toi que voilà qu'as-tu fait de ta jeunesse* ? God only knows. A snap of the fingers on a very idle pair of hands. To celebrate, I rode over to Felsöjattö, something I've always wanted to do. Right through Maroshely, down through miles of beet, to the place where the stream widens out, past the pretty church with the onion dome. At the end of the day I don't know which was the more stiff and exhausted, the horse or me. I used the saddle Papa ordered for himself when we were in London, without it I'd probably be a cripple. Twenty-four used to appear a mammoth age, when I would surely be grown-up. Actually I find I'm at one and the same time immeasurably old, and a child. I stayed with the von Pechys for a week over Christmas, very like old times. Winter stretches here so stark and stormy that you can't imagine it will ever end. The sky is inches off the earth. We live off the farm and the kitchen gardens very well. If alone, I eat with the Egyedys, I've grown fond of their two children, the girl especially, who has pigtails and gypsy eyes with which she flirts gravely. We're having a diet of black-pudding, having slaughtered the pigs, and I hear Rex saying, filthy foreign food. Kisch the upholsterer says he has followed your instructions exactly in replacing the curtains downstairs which finally fell to bits. Everyone likes what's been done, and you will too. Also we've taken the Isotta out of the garage, and are putting it back on the roads which is nice for someone who obviously is never to sit on a horse again.

24 May 1940, a postcard of Fisherman's Bastion in Budapest, with a view of the Danube below.

Im wunderschönen Monat Mai, Dein Jules.

2 September 1940.

The anniversary of the day when Adam was chased out of the garden for the second time. I wish I heard news of you. Something must be astray with our correspondence, you haven't answered my last three letters. Have you received them? Try a system of numbering so that I can be sure about what does and does not arrive. *Par les temps qui courent* we must be grateful for any communication, I do so much miss your advice and comfort. In particular I want you to be up to date about the factory. *Die Herren* are put out by its Venezuelan structure, Eduard has been here to explain how things are with them. It makes no real difference as far as production is concerned, of course, but they are sticklers for legality: isn't that nice? In a word, they are in the process of devising a way round by issuing shares of their own through directors they have appointed. Eduard argued that there was nothing to be done except ratify the plan, which is only one part of a much larger concept of theirs. Immense pressures are brought to bear on him, and to the extent that he has to live with *Die Herren* I sympathise, well, almost. His behaviour is equivocal, and I told him so. We should have nothing to do with the ins and outs of their squalid devices. If the ship must go down, as perhaps is the case, then its flag should fly to the end. Pernsdorf, according to him, is as it was. Burschen Franz is surviving. Eduard makes a point of being on good terms with Dr Huber, and dropping in regularly. One's mood alternates violently, not to say frighteningly, as these things sink in. Reading through the books here, I have picked up *Candide* and was swept along by its humour, absolutely relevant. 'I'd like to know which is worse, to be raped a hundred times by black pirates, to have a buttock cut off, to run the gauntlet among Bulgarians, to be whipped and hanged in an auto-da-fe, to be dismembered, to be a galley-slave, to undergo the miseries we all have known, or to stay here doing nothing.' The old gentleman might as well be grinning out of the window at Sans-Souci for a view of the march-past. Get Rex to read it again, the book captures his philosophy. Still it is Margulies and his wife that I can't get over, such pitiful deaths. And now number your letters, redouble your writing-output, Comrade Mother.

15 February 1941 (a letter numbered 'Six').

Nothing from you for ages. Fog creeps up to the windows, and demoralisation with it. Sometimes I think this flat and mournful winterscape is idyllic, 'a sea-coast in Bohemia' you might say, at other times I seem to revolve in small circles in some danger of spinning off at the edge of the horizon – except that there is no such thing as horizon right now, only vapour as white as wool.

Alas, they're been felling lots of the old trees, it can't be helped. Softwoods. If ever summer comes, it will be unsightly. Egyedy has had a lingering 'flu, but is recovering. I gave lazy oafish Dr F. a piece of my mind, in return for which he refuses to dish out any medicine. Professor Reischl has been here, very gloomy, sees no outcome to anything. Coughing like an old sheep too. News from home not promising. Toni writes that he hopes to come through Vienna, and if he makes it here, I'll know more. If I leave this sanctuary I spend all my time in queues. Geza has come to the rescue again. Touch and go, but everything is in order as far as permissions and passports are concerned, for the present anyhow. These things sap the spirit. I long to be with the two of you, to turn over a new page, to seize a stick and go for a walk on the kind of turf which exists only over there. Red brick, thatch, honeysuckle, hollyhocks, I see it all and for your sake I am truly thankful. Sorry to sound depressed. Perhaps when the fog clears we'll find that the lilies of the valley are out already. But write, *pour l'amour de Dieu*, dozens of letters, some are bound to arrive.

Some eight weeks after the date of that last letter, the German army crossed through Hungary in order to invade Yugoslavia, and the prime minister, Count Teleki, made it a point of honour to shoot himself. And the fog did not clear – if Jules was not using the expression in a literal sense, but rather as a thinly concealed code, a metaphor. Soon he had disappeared into it.

'Why not have made the effort to get away, to save himself? This Endre Schuster, for example, couldn't he have gone to Turkey with him, or on to Eretz Israel?'

'We shall never know,' Henriette replies.

Turning his back on his home, on life. A young man standing at the Sagodvar halt, nervous in manner, accustomed to protection, an artist. Brooding on the judgements of Professor Reischl who had no hopes, of Eduard von Arnheim, Toni Revertella, brooding on Dr Huber, the usurper. I reach out to him, pull him by the jacket, carry his leather suitcase, because it is madness to move in that direction. Suicide. These letters say everything and nothing. Between their lines, in all that loneliness, in all that vividness, is the face of Litzi, the woman he cannot bring himself to mention to his mother. Litzi is beseeching him, she weeps, she loves, punishes, crawls, insults; her eyes are shut and her mouth is open, filling with earth. The trains are waiting, unheated, jolting through provincial stations. There comes a border. Inspection of the passengers and their documents. Always inspections, always searches, always arrests. More and more trains are marshalling in the yards. Out of the fog looms Prince Paul Solkovsky, in the breeches and polished boots of his uniform. Iron on iron, the train wheels drum. I spend all my time in queues, he writes, these things sap the spirit. Naked, in a fake bathhouse, lacerating his pianist's hands on the cement ceiling and walls for a number of minutes in the throes of death. In queues, in another train, in another transport, soon Litzi will be passing. Where are they buried? Where? Who is with a wreath at that grave-side?

·Thirty Eight·

Pernsdorf, when I went there, was heat-stricken at the close of the long summer of 1961. A thunderstorm refused to break. Behind clouds piled high and livid shone a blotted mauve sun. The sultriness was uncomfortable, as I had to walk unexpected distances to find a place I supposed that I could identify from hearsay but which was in fact quite different. Not only the iron gate with the grille but the lodge itself had been dismantled, and the former main approach to the house has been altogether lost, incorporated in a newly built street. Another drive has been made to pass at the back, around a church which consists of slabs of cement propped and jutting at irregular angles and slopes, all of it topped by a shiny metal pole which spikes twenty or thirty feet of sky.

Pernsdorf today belongs to the Austrian trades union movement, and is used for conferences and seminars, or as just a good address for prominent union members and their guests. Fifteen years have passed since Henriette sold the property, and it has been municipalised beyond recognition. The park has disappeared so completely that it is impossible to decide quite where the lake was or where Rudi's ashes were scattered, or the position of the ancestral copper-beech in the photograph taken on Henriette's eighteenth birthday. The lawns on which Burschen Franz had laid out the tea-table are an expanse of gravel.

Only the house and its silhouette would be recognisable to Baron Gustav. Where the roof has been repaired, the recent slates have none of the weathering and hue of the old. A plate-glass swing-door has been installed. The refitted dome allows in a great deal more light. The stairs sweep up out of the hall, and in the place of the picture of the Arab prince and his retinue is suspended a roller map showing the representation and numbers of trades unions throughout Austria, with explanatory charts and statistics in lettering a foot high. Every wall is painted cream, on every floor lies matting. The main drawing-room has been converted into a lecture hall complete with platform, at whose rear is a curtained screen for slides. Zinc coffee machines; the stacked trays and food display-units and roped-off walk-ways of a self-service counter. In the canteen that day, places had been laid for at least a hundred diners, perhaps twice as many. The tables are plastic with cherry-coloured surfaces, and the chairs are in tubular chrome. In what had been the office where Baron Gustav and Henriette had supervised the accounts, with Margulies and Leviseur and Brühl, stands a television set, and wooden armchairs in a semi-circle around it. The library contains socialist magazines and periodicals, a couple of khaki filing cabinets, half a dozen varnished desks with no readers or researchers at them.

The director occupies Henriette's bedroom; young as he is, his cropped hair gives him a prematurely middle-aged appearance. Rimless spectacles; a leather jacket with a zip right up to the neck. Publicity packages are being prepared from separate piles of paper all over his desk and spreading to aluminium shelving. In what had been Henriette's bathroom a secretary darts around, ticking names off mailing-lists, seizing a hand-out here, a roneo-ed sheet there, adding to a little avalanche of material blocking up by the door.

'You're with the youth delegation from Klagenfurt? You are making sure to be in time for the dinner.'

The director pushes at the spectacles slipping down the bridge of his nose.

'My name is Julius Hechter.'

A copy of the evening programme is put into my hands. The guest of honour is to be Dr Plattkammer. The *résumé* of his career, I cannot help noticing, contains no mention of what he was doing between 1938 and 1945.

Fifty years in the movement, Dr Plattkammer is being

awarded a national decoration. The Minister of Labour, no less, is to be present and will make a speech, and afterwards the under-secretary at the Ministry is to give a formal address as well.

'You'll find it very rewarding,' the director says.

'My great-grandfather built this house, that's why I'm here.'

The director is politeness itself, he listens, he nods, he suddenly shakes my hand as if to formalise the introduction.

'Some of the locals talk about the Ellingen Schloss to this day,' he says, 'Let me fetch it out, we've some interesting literature about it.'

In the end it is the secretary who uncovers a leaflet, of four sides, much of which consists of photographs of the interior as now constituted. The leaflet is a pale shade of orange, the printing italicized. 'In 1889 Baron Ellingen, whose manifold capitalistic activities included the expansion of the state railway network and steel-making, purchased the estate. The present Schloss was his design, based upon plans by Siccardsburg and van der Null, architects of the Burgtheater. Few bourgeois houses were so elaborate. After Baron Ellingen's death, the house and grounds were purchased by the labour movement acting through its trades union representatives. In accordance with our principles and also with the urgent needs of reconstruction, the grounds have been developed to provide housing and facilities for eight hundred and twenty three families.'

So much for Henriette and her single family.

Delighted to show me round, the director accompanies me to the rooms upstairs, along the corridors where Jules had raced.

Dormitories now. 'Of course we could do with a bit more space really,' the director explains, 'so much is going on, but there it is, you can't have everything in life. The staircase,' he adds, 'is wonderful, historic.'

'Our modernisation has been thoroughly in keeping with the character here.' Self-praise comes naturally to the man.

Where once the garden had been, a hostel has been extended, in prefabricated wooden sections between house and stables, to accommodate visiting parties. The Klagenfurt youth delegation has actually arrived, beds are being allocated, knapsacks distributed from the bus. A special concern, so the director reassures me, is to spread their ideas and principles among the young. Training and teaching youth is a most welcome duty. Was I sure that I would not be attending the banquet in the evening? Dr Plattkammer, the Minister, the under-secretary – he promised to introduce me as an honoured visitor to these busy and distinguished men. Perry's Ridge: he wrote down the address, he would be contacting Henriette in the hope of an exchange of information.

'You must go and see it for yourself,' Oscar Webber had said. 'Spend six months there, a year, as long as you need. Become a witness, write a book, find a way to provide a grave for your parents.'

'If that's what you want,' Henriette said, 'I certainly shan't be the one to stand in your way. Speaking for myself, I never want to see or hear of any of them again as long as I live. I sold everything I could as soon as I could, I have no links. Except for our burial vault. I paid a sum to have that tended in perpetuity. They should be back quite soon asking for perpetuity all over again.'

The day on which I visited the Zentralfriedhof also happened to be the day when the delayed thunderstorm broke at last. An elemental sky and a rising wind almost made me cancel the journey out there, but it was the week-end. The procedure is to announce yourself to the supervisor in a central administrative office; to declare the name and religion of the deceased; upon which he looks up the number of the plot, with instructions for locating it in that cemetery. The walk is through tumbled rows and mounds, groupings of miniature chapels and chantries, until the inscriptions change from German into Hebrew. Weiss, Guttmann, Schey, Koenigs-warter, and Gustav Ellingen – the Jewish barons are together. Railings have rusted, stone has cracked and split, pieces of fallen masonry are grassed over. Gustav's bust has been smashed off, presumably for plunder.

Warm drops of rain cracked like bullets on my clothes. Out of an afternoon suddenly as darkened as dusk, thunder rolled, and above the city in the distance the lightning blazed: omens, if ever there were. Then a gale lashed the rain down. Trees were no shelter. I ran to a memorial with a colonnade around it, to crouch under one of its arches, with the water splashing off it. Under the force of the storm, puddles were forming instantly in the depressions of that summer-hardened earth.

Of Concordia, nothing has remained, no mark at all, not even the house in which Baron Gustav had his private quarters. On the terrain, in tremendous array, stand the glistening tanks of Austria's largest oil terminal.

Henriette had agreed with Oscar. 'I'll pay the hotel bill,' she had said, 'and your expenses. But please leave the von Arnheim woman out of it, her tongue is an automatic machine for telling lies.'

I had assumed that I would have only to tour the sites associated with Baron Gustav, and the past would become familiar. The name would be in hundreds of indexes, I thought, his life and times must emerge in the form of a biography, spontaneous and coherent. The search for Gustav has taken place in libraries, in rooms thickly smelling of dust where forms have to be filled in and hours pass and attendants far too bored to utter a word eventually push along trolleys full of reading matter.

But the Schlesinger Bank has left hardly more than its name. Lists of subscribers to concessions for new railway lines were published and the name of Ellingen crops up in them, but the commercial and financial process whereby the concessions were granted and the lists filled remains obscured. The crash of 1873, surely a tempting subject for economic or social historians, has been amazingly ignored, there is no standard work on it. Gustav's rise to success at the time depends for confirmation upon articles in the *Neue Wiener Tagblatt*, whose tone veers between malice and admiration. Not even Concordia has been studied, in spite of the fact that the factory's technical innovations are singled out here and there in specialist papers and journals, and its role in the industrial expansion of the Habsburg empire is praised. The elder von Arnheim, for instance, was responsible for building the first Siemens-Martin oven outside Germany. I have read von Kralik, and Goldhammer, and F. G. Steiner and Salo Mayer, I have checked Comte Vassili and Pater Gschwandt. Oberst Jantsch catalogues the stud-breeding and horse-racing in tedious detail. It is easier to learn facts about Kismet than Baron Gustav. I have wandered into forgotten scandals concerning Ritter von Ofenheim, accused of corruption as a rival railway builder, and also concerning the racist and nationalist Georg von Schoenerer, son of yet another railway developer. That was the climate in which Gustav operated, but of the man himself there remains not much more than Henriette and her legacy of anecdotes, the few intimate possessions rescued in Perry's Ridge.

Even the Waisenhaus has left no physical trace. The district was heavily shelled towards the end of the war, and has been rebuilt on a different street-grid. The very address cannot be established. The record of the orphanage's closure, however, exists in the collection of historical papers and documents maintained by the Jewish community. The entire archive is housed in two rooms in the house next to the synagogue. The place is musty with disuse. The curator is pleased to be of service, to have a request with which to deal. We are the living dead, his expression seems to say, all the Jews here were murdered but we were overlooked. He also appears to have memorised not just the location of every single piece of paper but its contents too. The Waisenhaus is known to him. A yellow file is fetched. On its cover the writing is old-fashioned *Schrift*, clerkly and correct, underlined with a ruler. Frau Ostersetzer, the archivist says, yes he recalls the name. She died, he thinks, in 1942, the details are in the folder of the Mohapelgasse Kinderheim.

The paper in the two folders is crumbling at the edge, fading brown. German typing was rather poor, carbon copies are hard to decipher. At 9.35 on the morning of 2 February 1940, it is noted, Dr Huber arrived at the Waisenhaus, and accompanying him was Obersturmführer Crevenek. A memorandum explains that on behalf of the community, Dr Löwenherz assembled the children in the street as fast as possible in order to evacuate within the hour, as instructed. Alternative accommodation for the children was arranged in the Kinderheim on the Mohapelgasse, another Jewish home, and accordingly the children were marched there. Cases or parcels larger than the tolerated measurements of eighty centimetres by seventy were confiscated by men from Crevenek's Gestapo detachment. Dr Löwenherz undertook to guarantee that the city's public services would be put to no extra expense by the move. A copy of the Waisenhaus requisition order, duly signed by Crevenek, is appended to the file. In his annual report for 1942, the director of the Mohapelgasse Kinderheim mentions that the illness and death of Frau Ostersetzer has been a serious set-back to their work. At least she died in hospital. The Kinderheim too was closed, on 2 May 1943, when the Mohapelgasse children were deported, all of them to be murdered in Auschwitz.

On the way from the hotel to the Staatsbibliothek is the Graben, the Kohlmarkt, then the Michaelerplatz, where on the third floor of a nondescript stuccoed house are the windows of what once was Rudi's flat, and in which Jules celebrated his twenty-first birthday. Towards the upper part of the house, at a point where an adjoining roof slopes down towards it, a tablet has been fixed on the wall to the effect that the poet Metastasio stayed there almost two centuries ago. A historic house, then, a house with cosmopolitan and artistic associations. When did the lease fall in, I wonder, and in what circumstances and by what right did subsequent possessors occupy the flat? The shutters once were grained but have lapsed to a shabby brown, and behind them took place the affair between Rudi and Jacques Chauzal. Up there, Henriette and Louise von Arnheim stripped the bed in the hysterical search for evidence, and the relationship with Rex no doubt was also decided in those rooms. There is no lobby for a concierge, even if Frau Kohak had not long since departed.

An altered entrance has been set back from the pavement, it is approached down a short enclosed alley, in the form of an airless courtyard, suffocating with the stench of night-cats.

·Thirty Nine·

Those who grew up under the Hitler regime can be recognised at a glance. Even in civilian clothes, they wear their experience as distinctly as a uniform. Discipline, the square shoulders seem to proclaim; *Dienst ist Dienst* is the message of those dogged faces, with a self-contained and shut-in dryness to them, as much as to say that the inner secret is there all right, stubbornly retained and impenetrable.

'Terrible times.'

Heinz, the son of Burschen Franz, drops the phrase with a prolonged sigh into any suitable pause of the conversation.

'Dreadful things happened, oh yes indeed they did, quite unimaginable to the likes of us,' he says, shaking his head in a way which refers the general harm to himself.

'Hitler was the devil incarnate.'

At the remark, Traudl, his wife, slips a good deal of anxiety into her smile, and some apology too.

As small men sometimes do, Heinz looks younger than his age. All good humour and bustle, the admirable cheerfulness of knowing that he has always done his duty. His hair is still cropped; no side-burns. Fresh colour in his cheeks. And if those times were terrible, he loves to talk about them, the man comes alive when he reminisces, a smile of true pleasure settles on his face, not conscious that here might be an obstacle to a relationship. He looks sideways at Traudl and laughs aloud at the memory of the friendliness of the French, their food, the pretty girls and especially Mademoiselle Francine and her two sisters. To have been stationed in Normandy was the best time of his life. *Und Paris, na ja, eine Weltstadt* – it must be the most beautiful city in the world, and he saw it at its finest, calm and orderly without traffic. If only there hadn't been the accident, but he taught himself to write with his left hand, and even that worked out to his advantage.

Traudl has the reticence long ago indoctrinated into members of the *Bund der Deutschen Mädchen*. To this day, she avoids make-up, and her face is very well preserved, not to say smooth. Right in the front of her mouth is a silvery tooth, which somehow seems a certificate of her modesty. The unshaven hair on her legs can be seen black and streaky under her stockings. 'We had special little frocks,' she says. 'We plaited our hair with ribbons for the parades, it was the highlight of the week. The neighbours participated, we knew them all, such a spirit of friendliness has been lost.'

'Continue, please sing the songs, she remembers all the verses.'

But Traudl only grimaces a little, pulling down the corners of her mouth, as he adds that with a voice like hers she could have been a singer, in a choir, and who knows, in the opera.

Heinz has risen in the world. He is a quality supervisor for the largest chocolate manufacturer in the country. He drives a Volkswagen. Their apartment is on the ground floor of a comfortable block in expensive brick. The place is spotless, every surface polished. Their married son is away in Indonesia erecting telephone poles and cables for an international company. Inge, the nineteen-year-old daughter, lives at home in a thicket of carefully cherished dolls and knick-knacks, as well as books of the useful sort, such as encyclopedias. Attending a course at a school for design, she makes clothes for herself and her mother. When she is at home, the sewing-machine stutters away obediently in the corner. The living-room contains an upright piano, in which Traudl takes pride, although the keyboard is scarcely touched except with a duster. In a favourite chair Heinz holds forth. Boxes of chocolates are within reach, so that he can offer them round, repeating a line about how he personally can vouch for them. To keep their figures, Heinz and Traudl are keen week-end walkers. It bothers them that I have refused to move into the bedroom vacated by the son in Indonesia.

Why waste good money on a hotel? I count as a member of

the family, do I not? Because they have known me since the dark days when the Russians were here, and that was practically the worst of the war.

'Every Christmas I send the Frau Baronin a card, and she always replies.'

Heinz opens doors for Traudl, he stand up eagerly when she enters with coffee, and again when she carries out the tray of dirty cups. In return for attentiveness, she makes sure that conversation is led where he wants.

'Terrible about Baron Jules, poor young man. So nice, he was, Father spoke of him with tears in his eyes. You'd never have believed such things were possible.'

Left to himself, Heinz would prefer to dwell on his comrades and their humours and successes, not just the girls and horse-play either, but their real friends, cultured people, the lawyer at Pont-à-Voyren, for instance, the genial schoolmaster at Moyssac.

But I have questions, and he would not dream of dodging them. Yes, he saw Huber. Well-spoken, he never raised his voice, not like some of them. An educated man. Say what you like, he looked after Pernsdorf as though it had been his own property, and Concordia too. Only once, in 1942 or perhaps 1943, had there been a party which had got a little out of control, with Party big-shots upstairs, men like the Gauleiter himself. Of course his old father had been pensioned off by then: well, not exactly pensioned.

Sometimes Heinz has a confidential manner. It is easy to guess what he is about to say when he puts his hand on my arm, leans closer, lowers his voice.

'Father worked sixty-one years for the family. Man and boy. A life-time. His death was badly timed, I know, but that was no fault of his. He received no pension, no recompense. The family left it to the Nazis, the Nazis left it to the family, so he was caught in the middle. Here the custom is to rent a grave, I have to renew the rental for Father's grave. Would you put in a word for me, ask the Frau Baronin to purchase the plot outright, in lieu of a pension, a recompense? All things considered, the Frau Baronin would be delighted to put this right, especially if you were to ask on my behalf. Is that not so ?'

If terrible times happen by themselves, as though spontaneously, akin to acts of nature, then nobody is to blame for them. So it was with the Nazis, and then with the Reds and the Allies. So it was when the Frau Baronin cut her losses and sold Pernsdorf and the site of the factory. Look at the fabulous developments at both places. Think of the potential fortune she must have lost through short-sightedness, impatience, call it what you will.

'What about the stealing ? The house was looted bare.'

'I can put my hand on my heart,' Heinz says solemnly, 'and swear that I saw Amelie wearing the Frau Baronin's black fur coat. Much good it did her. She died that same year.'

'Louise von Arnheim took cognac. And anything else ?'

'The Frau Baronin's reactions are very understandable,' Heinz says, 'but bear in mind that she wasn't there, it is only natural to place the worst possible interpretation on things. Frau von Arnheim is an educated woman, no common thief or profiteer.' Family possessions had been packed off by the crate to England before the war. He himself had helped Frau von Arnheim to transport some of the remainder to Wasserburg. Safe-keeping, of course. Dr Huber turned a blind eye, he knew that the house and park were to be used for military purposes. Everyone lost their heads easily at that stage. Why, even Dr Huber volunteered for the front, and got himself killed. All very sad.

'Frau von Arnheim has played such a part in what I've heard that I should like to see her. It might not be welcome.'

'Well,' he says, 'we can only try to make peace, there's nothing wrong with that. I'm in contact with her, I'll ask, but you'd better be careful.'

Through the last of the hot weather and into the fall, I had been living in a hotel behind the Graben. A modern place, inexpensive. In their spare time, or on a Sunday, I went with Heinz and Traudl on occasional expeditions, to Klosterneuburg and the monastery at Melk, to the vineyards and wine-cellars of the Wachau. Once or twice I responded by taking

Inge to the cinema or to a restaurant. She will be a decent wife for someone. From her father she has heard so much about the fabulous city of Paris that her prime ambition is to spend a year there.

A narrow lobby leads up to the desk of that hotel. One evening I could hardly enter because of a row taking place. A man in a red check shirt was blocking the entrance. A taxi-driver, he was complaining that he had driven his client in from the airport but she was refusing to pay the fare. Beyond him stood the girl at whom he was shouting. Answering in fluent German, the girl was insisting that there was a good reason for not paying, the man had insulted her, the police should be fetched. 'What did he say?' I asked. That was for the police. 'Let's call them,' I told the concierge. The taxi-driver drove off so angrily that the tyres of his car whined on the asphalt.

Mira is a girl brought up under Mediterranean sun, she likes to wear white cotton to set off her summer colouring. A girl for beaches and swimming-pools, you might think at first glance, before paying attention to the look in her eyes, a look which is the assertion of someone both studious and decisive. At about the moment that I was reflecting that an elastic band tying back her dark hair into a pony-tail was rather spoiling an otherwise glamorous presence, I also noticed how she was keeping hold of a violin-case. Mira was in Vienna to attend a master-class.

'And what did the taxi-driver say that so upset you?'

'To repeat it is to spread the pollution.'

The concierge now discovered that there had been some muddle about Mira's reservation, and no room was available. I helped her to find somewhere else, I carried her suitcase. 'You'll see,' she said. 'That concierge heard the taxi-driver and he'll be making trouble for you before long.'

On account of Mira, I went to the conservatoire, and sat in the auditorium where Toscanini had paid his compliment to Jules. Musicians of the standing of Szerynk and Isaac Stern were in circulation. At those master-classes, Mira had friends, fellow-violinists, a couple of Americans, and a Swede who was a hypochondriac and carried his own hand-towel to the wash-room, to save himself from possible contamination. Cheap tickets could be obtained to concerts and the opera. We used to meet up afterwards over meals in cellars below former palaces.

'Your researches are important,' Mira said. 'We have to learn what the Germans really think of us, what really they think they did to us. If Louise von Arnheim doesn't want to see you, you'll have to force your way in. You must have the information. The right to have it is also yours, never mind what anyone says to the contrary.'

The address which Heinz had given me for Louise von Arnheim proved to be an old people's home, far away beyond the end of the Döblinger Hauptstrasse, where the city peters out into new sprawl. A site of several acres contains flats, a school, a crèche, suitable trees and the requisite statues to promote kindness and universal peace. Blank walls have been adorned with pastoral scenes of hay-making and herding, or else carry pieces of abstract iron-work for purposes of culture.

A door like a gigantic brick cave led into the home. On the first floor was an immense gallery of a day-room into which perhaps a hundred wheel-chairs had been collected and aligned. Each had been pushed into positions along the entire length of the two facing walls, and secured there. A wooden bar, with tray attached, was lowered from wall-fixings over the head of each person, effectively locking them one and all into their wheel-chairs. Several had slumped down. A few were mumbling to themselves and weeping. Although it was not a cold day, the central heating had already been turned on, and an oily roasting arose from the pipes and radiators.

Part of the picture of Louise in old days before the break with Henriette had been drawn in Viennese clichés of vivacity and frivolity, all blond curls and smiles. Here she was in a cubicle of her own, crouched in a chair, with a rug over her knees. Ill and poor. She looked years older than Henriette. White hair cut short, and thin. Her eyes levelled at me with a flair of animal intelligence in them. On her hands were a pair of mittens, and she stroked the tips of her fingers over the faded wool.

'I know who you are, Heinz has told me, that man's a goose. Why should I agree to see you?'

She told me to leave in a way which made it plain that she realised that a little moment of power might have been offered her, and she was not going to waste it. I sat down.

'You've come to spy, to gloat. I haven't a groschen, the Gemeinde looks after me, I'm entirely at the mercy of the people here. It's an alms-house. No pension, nothing. Eduard's work was good enough to bring me to this room. You go and tell your grandmother that.'

'She doesn't know I'm here.'

'She will.'

In that cubicle, its walls an institutional beige, were a radio, a hot-water bottle, a pair of spectacles, otherwise nothing personal. A library book about the Habsburgs lay face down on the bed.

'The grandson, the famous grandson,' she said. 'Who turned up as a surprise at the end of the war. Another foundling. Illegitimacy runs in the family. And to which side do you belong,' she asked, 'the self-made and unrespectable Ellingens, or the pompous Hechters standing on their dignity? And what you know about me is that I'm a thief, isn't that so? Well have a good look round at the fruit of it.'

'What most concerns me,' I said, 'is why Jules did so little to save himself. As if Rex had put him under sentence of death.'

'So what can I tell the famous grandson, your mind is closed shut. You young people are all alike, all you want to know is who went to bed with whom, and when and why and how it was. Yes I told her about Rudi, to her face, because I realised that he never spent a night with her. The homosexual as family man, it's a complete fantasy. She married them one after another out of self-assertion and the need to dominate, to be an Ellingen like her father. Now he *was* somebody. By comparison every man she met was a disappointment, and that spoilt Rudi especially despicable. Like a fish with a hook in its mouth. A wet blanket, he could ruin any pleasure. Of course she should have been a man herself. And while we're on the subject of physical relationships, let me tell you that Rudi soon regretted introducing Rex into the house but couldn't see how to push him out. "One doesn't introduce that kind of man into one's family," he used to complain. "At least Jacques Chauzal was well-bred." "You chose him," I answered, "you want him, you live with him. Leave us out of it." But Henriette had them both in her power, didn't she, and that was what she really enjoyed, probably she never enjoyed anything except manipulating. Money like hers is power, she realised that somebody was going to have to support Rex. In England they still send pansies to prison, isn't that so? The one died broken-hearted, and the other probably didn't have a heart to break.'

'I don't know whether you are also in her power,' Louise von Arnheim continued, 'but if so, then you'll be destroyed as surely as both those husbands, and Jules too. Not to mention me. One thing you can be sure of, she'll never give you a single groschen.'

Walking back through that long gallery of old people pinioned helplessly in wheel-chairs, I had a sense of truth as an element of deception, shrivelling and dying at the touch.

'The woman's bitterness,' I wrote to Henriette, 'will keep her alive for years.' This is the answer I received:

Beloved Boy, It distresses me to think of you in a room of your own by yourself. Nowhere can be lonelier than that capital of so-called *Gemütlichkeit*. I was miserable so often. Awful people, *falsch und mies*, they flatter you to your face and behind your back invent the most spiteful things they can. I have transferred money to your account so you are free to do as you like, but why not come home at the end of the year? The evidence you need is in the house here, if really you would write a portrait of my father. Since you refused to follow my advice, you can hardly complain if you find the von Arnheim so odious. That's Viennese back-biting at its worst, whatever she may say is just so much poison dripped into your ear, distortions, pleading, outright lies and slanders. Quite simply, she was mad with jealousy. She put me through the worst scene of my life. People of that sort only pretended to be our friends so that they could squeeze out of us whatever they could. Haven't you noticed that what it comes down to, with the whole pack of them, is that they want more money which they know quite well they don't deserve ?

·*Forty*·

Mira's predictions had been right : the hotel concierge made me feel unwelcome, he suppressed telephone messages, spoke of heavy extra bookings, began to ask for payment in advance. I heard of a flat to rent on a monthly basis in a house behind the Franziskanerplatz. A bedroom, a living-room, a kitchen, at the very top of the building. Six flights of steep stairs were provided with a wooden hand-rail and a system of electric lighting which switched itself off, always too soon, to leave one in the dark between one floor and the next. High enough above the streets to have a fine view of the roof-tops around the Franziskanerkirche, the place seemed to belong to another and more secret world. Living there, I had something like a resident's encounter with the city.

Mira is only a few years older than me. Her family had emigrated from Germany on the eve of the war, and she grew up in Jerusalem. Her father is an agricultural expert, a consultant for one of the United Nations agencies, and it is a kind of hobby of his to telephone from the unlikeliest places, to send post-cards and even money-orders, as though to test the world's capacities for communications. He bought her the violin she plays, an old instrument with a light and glowing patina, which reminded me of her own beautiful and sensuous skin.

'The place where really I was born,' Mira says, 'is in the Mendelssohn violin concerto, the bar where the solo takes off.'

With six weeks of her master-class still to go, Mira moved into the flat with me. Nothing is quite like first love. We had the holiday season at the end of the year more or less to ourselves. For Mira's sake, I carried logs of wood up those endless stairs, so that after dark, we could build up a fire in the grate. Before going to bed, she used to practise whatever piece it might be, and I can see her now in her night-dress, barefoot on the carpet, her head to one side, and the flames of the fire dying behind her. An expression of remoteness, almost puzzlement, sometimes crosses her features, as though she were staring abstractedly at her own talent. At the conclusion of the master-class, she played a sonata, and her success could be sensed gathering like a storm due to burst.

'You'll come to us,' she said, or rather promised. 'You'll stay in our house, then you won't be able to leave. There's nowhere we can live except in our own country, among ourselves. Maybe it's wrong to be so nationalistic but when I play I feel I do so for our people.'

'Somebody one day will understand,' she said, 'but first they need facts. You have this Paul Solkovsky's address in Munich, make an appointment and confront him. Why wait? Never mind what your grandmother thinks. He doesn't pretend not to know what was happening at Theresienstadt. If you could grasp how it was possible to catch sight of Jules going to his death and still do nothing, you might reach the mystery of German behaviour in the Hitler period.'

In the new year, it was arranged that Mira would meet her father in Frankfurt. An only child, she accommodates to his whims and surprises. First Munich, then, and afterwards Frankfurt. We hired a car in a week of odd and unpredictable weather, when snow was falling in flurries which either instantly melted away or at night froze into black ice. The crimson scarf which I had given Mira was wrapped over her head and around her ears, and its ends tucked into her coat, giving her the look of a girl in a Russian novel. She hugged her violin case.

On the German *autobahn*, a green road-sign points to Dachau. The name is proclaimed in the largest lettering, as though it were quite normal. Carpenters had recently restored the concentration camp, and surrounding wire and watchtowers, the huts. More than authentic, the place was in working order. On that late afternoon, under lowering snow-clouds, men and women were stepping out of a number of buses. Condensation steamed over the bus windows. Drinks had been served on board. The men were stout in lined winter jackets and lace-up boots or snow-shoes, they rubbed their hands, they bellowed at one another and lit cigars, they escorted broad-hipped women. Pensioners, they were on a seasonable outing to a place where all or any of them might have served as licensed murderers.

'And if Solkovsky is like this,' Mira asked, 'what will you do?'

'It comes to me,' I said, 'that he and Jules once played a duet together, but it wasn't a success. Solkovsky fancied himself as a cellist.'

In Munich we visited the Pinakothek and the Glyptothek, we saw the Feldherrnhalle. Solkovsky's face started to haunt me, I imagined him like a skull with a death's head grin, and carrying a Nazi war veterans' pin in the lapel of his jacket; his old army peaked-cap on a hat-stand in the entrance; a photograph of him with General Schaer and the officers of the 117th Infantry Division.

On the following morning, the appointment with Solkovsky was for ten o'clock. 'Please have lunch or dinner with me at your convenience,' the man had written in the correspondence leading up to this meeting. Hospitality from him: it was unthinkable.

'I'll wait for you in the car,' Mira said, 'and if you're not down by one o'clock, shall I come up?'

A maid opened the door. There was no hat-stand, no military souvenirs. I was ushered down a long corridor with a tapestry along one side of it. Prince Paul Solkovsky was in a grey flannel suit, with suede shoes, a silk tie and handkerchief to match. When he stood up, I saw that he had a stoop. Though he was mostly bald, some hair straggled from his forehead across his scalp and its wisps made him seem decrepit. The hand he held out was as cold as if he had been out of doors.

'Your grandmother has written to me, look, here's her letter. She tells me you are anxious to learn about your family and its antecedents.'

Round the walls of the room are the portraits of ancestors which he had managed to salvage from the great hall at Rentzenburg. Also a collection of porcelain, on brackets or in a pair of cabinets lit from within. He begins to tell a long and complicated story about how he rescued these possessions and brought them away here. I feel myself losing control, a knot of tension forming in the pit of the stomach. The man has no conception of what is being asked of him.

'Very few people can still be alive who can call on a clear memory of Baron Gustav,' he says, 'and I must be among the last. I was in his box when Kismet won that wonderful race. Only as a small boy, of course, brought along by my father. Carstairs the jockey laughed out loud when he was given the prize money. Funny what one remembers. Baron Gustav used to smell very strongly of some special lotion he ordered from London. Wasn't that the height of elegance?'

'You are also the last of his friends to have seen Jules alive.'

The man speaks slowly, and the words are carefully chosen, over the years the arguments have evidently been rehearsed and refined.

'We Germans will have to do penance for five hundred years and more,' he says. 'The nation has to answer for its crimes. That's clear. But each one of us cannot sit in sackcloth and ashes. You, my young friend, are speaking as a citizen of a world in which you decide what to do and what not to do, and you alone will be responsible for the consequences. But you cannot judge us according to such fortunate standards. I could no more have stepped forward to save Jules than he could have stepped out of the column towards me. Hitlerism was dictating to us both.'

'It was not the face of Hitlerism he carried to Auschwitz, but yours. The face of an individual from whom he had every reason to expect friendship.'

'But the friendship had already been betrayed by the mere fact that the Nazis were in power. Our mutual fates had long since been settled. You are as cruel as the Nazis if you want us to have been exceptional. Ordinary folk aren't supermen, they don't become heroes on demand, they don't martyr themselves either. How would it have helped if the guards had shot Jules on the spot for attempting to escape? Had I made a martyr of myself, how would that have helped him?'

Actually he pities himself, probably started doing so on the very afternoon when Jules and the column disappeared into the fortress prison of Theresienstadt, to leave behind a stain on his conscience. Push that logic to its conclusion, and it was Jules who did him the injury by being in the column. If the prisoners had all been anonymous, he could have driven home with General Schaer comfortably congratulating himself on not being one of the brutish guards, quite untainted by what he'd come a long way to observe.

'You weren't humanitarians when you drove off to witness what was happening at Theresienstadt. On the contrary, you were turning yourselves from passive into active accomplices. Just because you weren't directly involved, you could allow yourselves to feel stand-offish, morally better. It would be quite enough to be able still to shudder at the sight. Jules proved your complicity, though that was beyond anything you could have guessed beforehand, I concede. You might not have been a martyr either, but an example to millions who were waiting for a lead from men in your position.

'And another thing. Once, in a room of your castle, with these very same pictures on the walls, you'd lost your temper in a duet with Jules, just because he was the more talented. Your revenge happened to be in that column, only you hadn't anticipated how personal it would be, nor the enormity of it. That's the reason why you were confused.'

He picks his way along the train of thought in silence for a while, bending his arm at the elbow in a reflex gesture somewhere between repudiation and defence, only to begin a sentence about the definition of complicity in those circumstances, and then he stops as the door swings open. A girl enters noisily. About my age. His daughter. She dumps a shoulder-bag and a raincoat on to a chair. She offers me a cup of coffee, or tea if I would prefer. She also asks where I am staying, how I am enjoying Munich, whether I have a programme. A group of her university friends is apparently about to gather in a café in Schwabing. Impatience shakes me, I stand up to leave, with a sense that we have been trapped for centuries already, and there is no penance.

Outside in the car is Mira, with her crimson scarf and her violin-case. I try to reproduce the conversation, to explain its futility after all this time in which the man has lost his hair and acquired a stoop and raised a daughter who offers me a programme for the rest of my stay.

Mira's father met us in Frankfurt. A cheerful, energetic man. In spite of the weather, we managed to enjoy ourselves before the two of them flew home. I had the address, I promised to visit them. At the airport I asked Mira one last time what that taxi-driver had said to upset her, so unwittingly bringing us together.

'Oh,' she replied, 'when he heard why I speak German, he swivelled round in his seat and his words were, So you got away, a pity, a mistake, next time we'll make sure to clean out the lot of you.'

Lately Mira has joined the international concert circuit. Sometimes I read of her successes and see a photograph of her. If I can claim to have done anything for Mira, my Mirele, it is to have made her wear her hair more loosely, no longer bunched in an elastic band. What the critics like to praise is her expressiveness, which is, they say, the product of a mature and rounded personality.

•Forty One•

'Place of birth given as Budapest, but yours is a British passport,' Stavrakis said on the telephone. 'I'll have it checked with the Foreign Office, in principle it should be all right. If it'll round off your researches, I could find time to drive with you to Sagodvar round about early March.

'You realise Henriette's worrying,' he said. 'She thinks you're not stable or secure enough for what you're putting yourself through.'

I knew. I could tell that if I were within reach it would have been a case of Dicky Harwood all over again. Mostly this was due to Paul Solkovsky's account of my conduct. In Henriette's eyes, he had long since exculpated himself: his confession to her after the war was convincing, and the writing of it had implied the receiving of her sympathy, if not pardon. Had not the final sight of Jules been the kind of coincidence on which nobody can reckon?

Henriette wrote repeatedly that I ought now to be preparing to go to a university. 'Even if you find these famous roots of yours, you can't live off them,' as she put it in one of her disconcerting phrases. Duly prompted, Oscar Webber also wrote to suggest that North Western might be the right college, unless I preferred Chicago itself.

Stavrakis as emissary; Stavrakis as fixer. Even in Vienna, he was able to round up a party. Like his wallet, his address-book was in crocodile skin, and he turned its pages with one hand while at the same time sitting on the bed in his hotel room and using the telephone with the other hand. There was some woman whose name he had forgotten, and this irritated him. His friends, it appeared, were meeting later in the evening to play roulette.

On the morning when we drove out of the city centre, rain had started to fall. There were no reliable petrol-stations in Hungary, according to Stavrakis, so we had first to buy jerry-cans and fill them.

He said, 'Sagodvar before the war, those really were the good old days. There's no fun like that left anywhere in the world, perhaps it was too good to last. We were rather rough on the girls, I'm sorry to tell you, hoping to make the grade as Don Juans.'

'I used to calm Jules down,' Stavrakis explained. 'What bothered him emotionally was to learn the truth about his father. Seeing how his worship of his father had a completely false basis. I mean, what must it have been like to have your father seducing your tutor? Or the other way around, which-ever it was. He was beside himself, he became so upset. He used to tell me about how he was going to smash Rex's teeth down his throat, throw him out of the window and all that.'

'And was that why he went to Sagodvar and just gave up? It's as if he couldn't bring himself to go on staying alive. Unless Litzi had something to do with it.'

'Litzi I never knew. But I used to say to him, what does it matter to you if they're pansies? Being queer isn't inherited, it doesn't go from one generation to another like congenital syphilis. But nobody likes being teased, especially on subjects of that kind. There was something in Jules, I guess, that wanted to get things over and done with.'

Stavrakis has his loyalties; when I press him further, he will only shrug, uncharacteristically non-committal. And how are Henriette's motives to be understood? Did she in fact exact revenge on her husband for his homosexuality by first stealing away, and then marrying, his lover, or was she colluding in the whole business, and lesbian? 'Of course she should have been a man', in the words of Louise von Arnheim.

The Iron Curtain was reached at Hegyeshalom. A huge wire fence ran through the countryside, with manned watch-towers at regular intervals. A red-and-white pole had been lowered across the deserted road. No other car was crossing. The police held automatic weapons under their waterproof capes. The black sports car was itself a challenge, and sure enough, everything had to be unpacked and opened. The jerry-cans of petrol, Stavrakis had to repeat more and more emphatically, were not for sale on the black market.

Kapusvar, Gyor: the drab towns were rainsoaked. Potholes everywhere, and ducks or geese unaccustomed to giving way to traffic. Now and again a passing lorry splashed a muddy spray over the windscreen. I read the map.

'And this girl you've been living with, she really matters to you? She's already married, but to a violin. You wouldn't want that for the mother of your children.'

The road turned through Maroshely, past the church with the onion dome. Then Zalaszentistvan, with the fields ploughed in long dark strips on the approach to Sagodvar.

'Here we are arriving and speculating about a girl,' Stavrakis said, '*Plus ça change....*'

A postman was bicycling around the low houses. He stopped to stare, and was joined by a woman in a headscarf who had been sweeping dust out over her door-step with a broom of home-cut twigs. Where once the station had stood, and the carriages had waited for those arriving from Vienna, was a new village square of sorts, with buildings in brick, including a regional office of the Communist Party, its flag limp and dragging in the rain. The windows were boarded over on what had been the school built by Baron Gustav, with its telegraph office in the rear. Water had collected in the area in front of it, a mock-substitute for the missing village pond.

The surface of the road was disintegrating into a trail of mud. No avenues of trees now led to the house. Driving at a walking-pace, we came up to a huge expanse of yard, laid out in front of the former stables. Assorted trucks and lorries were parked there. Sagodvar has become a vehicle maintenance depot for the Hungarian army.

The tennis court has vanished under the tarmac; so has much of the garden. Where a grassy patch survives, stones from the animal cemetery have been reset as markers and kerbs, and one or two names can even be deciphered:

Kurban, Rustum, Coccinelle. No trace remains of the sheds or tracks of the estate train.

'That magnolia ought to be somewhere,' Stavrakis said. 'A girth like an elephant's, and branches sweeping down, you couldn't be spotted underneath. Once I had Irma Grunberger up against it. A really good-hearted creature, she helped out when she could.'

Life can be as inconsequential as any dream. A number of soldiers had gathered to admire Stavrakis's Porsche. We found ourselves escorted into the house, to confront an officer. A man in his shirt-sleeves, none too well shaven, he was sitting moodily at a desk on which was an ash-tray piled up with stubs of cheap cigarettes. Examining our passports, he noted the details. In German, we explained who we were and why we had come.

On the other side of the house, the French windows have been knocked out to install concrete pillars for garages extending over the old terrace. Where the drawing-room had been now rises a ramp into a work-shop. Lights were on there, an engine was suspended from a gantry and around it an instructor was evidently holding a class for fitters or mechanics.

Plenty of people in the village would apparently be able and willing to talk to us about pre-war days. Far from detaining us, the officer had buttoned his jacket, volunteering to be the interpreter. In a car of his own, he drove ahead to the square in the village. The inn had a low ceiling, its windows were closed, and the air was choking. Bread and sausages were fetched, and bottles of apricot brandy. The room filled. An elderly woman played her fingers across my face, establishing a family likeness. 'Eighty pounds of meat used to be supplied to the big house every week when Henriette was there,' the officer was reporting what someone at his elbow was telling him with urgency. 'If the *Herrschaften* left a week early or stayed on unexpectedly, the butcher's budgeting for the whole year might be affected.' There was another old lady who still washed her sheets in the same place in the stream, and every time she did so, she said, she thought of Frau Egyedy bringing down the laundry in wicker baskets on a cart. Someone else remembered how Jules had played the piano at the inn, which had made him popular; apparently he had been at all the dancing in the village. 'What, in this very room?' 'No, the previous inn-keeper had been in trouble, his place was closed down.' In Hungary five years after the national uprising of 1956, in the darkness of repression without end, I heard women saying, 'Your family will come back, you will live long enough to see that, don't lose hope.' 'Believe them,' the interpreter-officer added, 'it's true.' The brandy had gone rapidly to my head. I managed to force open one of the windows, and leant out into the damp night, giddy to be in the crowd of strangers, but wild and tipsy with the celebration of nothing at all. They left me to sleep on a sofa, and Stavrakis in the car.

Early next morning, Stavrakis was already himself, in a clean shirt with his initials embroidered on it, a cashmere sweater casually round his shoulders, his after-shave stronger than the fug in the inn.

The church at Maroshely is padlocked. Close up, the onion dome's corrosion can be seen; weeds are springing up at its base. Unforgotten violences live in these half-smashed villages and scrappy fields. Had there been the same lowering sky twenty years earlier when Jules had made his way to the station? 'Geza shot some partridges with me, *il est toujours tellement bon garçon.*' At Felsöjattö, on the steps of his house, Geza von Pechy had been shot by a Russian soldier who climbed out of a tank with his pistol in his hand. Afterwards the Russians dragged French furniture out of the house, and built a bonfire, and threw the corpse on to it. Felsöjattö has been converted into flats. Slates are sliding off the roof, the guttering has been stripped and water-stains disfigure the honey-coloured stone of a classical facade. A hundred yards from the house is a stand-pipe, and children stagger from it with a bucket of water in each hand.

And Egyedy: a counter-revolutionary, he was in the prison at Vac, and died there after eighteen months. 'Poor papa,' Margit Egyedy will say, 'when they arrested him he was in breeches and gaiters, his working clothes, and they refused to let him change into anything more suitable.'

It is a drive of eighty miles from Sagodvar to the small industrial town where Margit lives: more properly, a prefabricated assembly of factories and warehouses and pylons. She has been allocated two rooms on the eighth floor of one of the units of collective housing. A notice forbids use of the lift 'for technical reasons'. On the first floor, the sound of our footsteps brought a man to his door, to ask who we were proposing to visit. 'She's out,' he informed us. So she was.

'I eat with the Egyedys, I've grown fond of their two children, the girl especially, who has pigtails and gypsy eyes with which she flirts gravely,' Jules had written. Hardly forty, Margit has let herself go. She dresses untidily, she chain-smokes, and there is nothing the least flirtatious in those eyes.

'The man on the first floor must have watched you,' she says, 'He's our block warder, his boy helps him out.'

'Nothing will happen,' she assures us. 'Things are no longer what they were.' Her parents are dead but her father has been rehabilitated; she received a letter to the effect that it had been a mistake, or in their language 'an impermissible effort of social justice.' Two or three times a year, she travels to her brother, he has a job in a saw-mill. A translator by profession, she says that she is fortunate to have work of the kind when her class background is suspect. Properly educated, thanks to the sacrifices of her parents, she can translate from French, English and German, and she presents me with her latest publication, a Parisian thriller originally entitled *L'Assassin a raison*. The book has a smell of pulp-paper, it looks as if it must fall apart on being opened. On the fly-leaf, under her signature she writes, 'From one child of Sagodvar to another.'

Books are stacked up everywhere in the two rooms she occupies, they seem to have slipped down even on to the couch on which she sleeps. There is also a stove, but as far as can be seen, nothing to eat.

'Soon after the arrest of my father,' she says, 'Mother and I were forced out of Sagodvar. Of course the estate had already been confiscated, we realised we were vulnerable but tried to stay on. My parents had had a sense of right and wrong which was much too strong for their own good. We arrived here like refugees in our own country, all we had was a single suitcase between us. Mother couldn't bear it.'

'Why didn't you leave in 1956?'

'I have just as much right to be in this country as they do. The only time I've left the country was when we took you to the Frau Baronin after the war.'

I think to myself that there cannot be the least little aperture in her defences through which self-pity might trickle in, for then she would crack, dissolve under it. Her skin is hard and lined, as though attached to the underlying bone without benefit of flesh. The hair is short, in need of a comb.

Stavrakis is interrupting that it is eight o'clock and he must have a meal, we haven't eaten properly all day. Margit hesitates whether to accompany us. Sure enough, as we attempt to tiptoe clumsily past the informer on the first floor, his dog starts barking, and the door is flung open in our faces.

The empty streets of the town are stained yellowy-green under phosphorescent lamps. In the hotel where we are staying, the dining-room is blacked-out, shut. We appear to be the sole guests. Listening to us, the manager claims that we should have given instructions by mid-day at the latest, it is too late to unlock the kitchen now, he has no staff. If we are prepared to wait, he will see what can be done. An hour later, he returns with slices of bread and margarine, pickles, some brawn, and litre bottles of beer. The three of us sit with this food in the lobby. Overhead the lights ought to contain four bulbs, but only one has been screwed in, which has the effect of casting shadows rather than illuminating.

'Whatever makes you imagine that Litzi had flat shoes and a shabby coat,' Margit wants to ask. 'On the contrary she was well dressed. They were rather a fast set, I was young at the time and glamorised by all their comings and goings. The newest records on the gramophone, that kind of thing. Most of the crises were to do with Jules's papers, he needed permits of one sort or another. Another thing I remember is that you could hardly go into the house without hearing him play the same tune, over and over, he had it on the brain, something that sounded from a light operetta. Lonely, I suppose. He and my father certainly discussed what ought to be done for the best. One day he wasn't there, and another day you were deposited with us. The war was like that. It had been quite a charmed life up till then, in the countryside at least. People like Jules were so accustomed to having their way that they couldn't really believe in anything else. Sagodvar was isolated, out of things. My parents couldn't come to terms with that departure, they called Jules arrogant, and I understood what they meant only when it was our turn to face the communists. Arrogance isn't quite right, but no other word will serve. You have to show them what's what. Deep down, there's the urge to turn yourself into a living example. Even when fear takes control, there's exhilaration or excitement about it, at the same time to be doing what you have to, and to be sharing the experience of the masses.'

The sandwiches have been left uneaten; Margit has hardly sipped her beer. The hotel is deserted, we have the place to ourselves.

' "Litzi will come back as soon as she can," my parents said. "she'll want to fetch the child." They had an address for her. To be frightened wasn't in their nature, they were practical people, both my parents. Everybody respected them. Mother adored children too, she was happy to look after you. We read in the newspapers, where the round-ups and death-marches were reported, even boasted about, I'd say. Litzi knew what to expect by then, the Germans and the Arrow Cross made no secret of their plans. She'd done the right thing, bringing you to us, there couldn't be any doubt about that. We had other refugees, some of them were put into the big house. I well remember father telling us that Budapest was unrecognisable when at last he was able to get there, not a capital city any longer, after they'd fought over it to the very end. Nobody was at that address. He couldn't make headway. Seideler, it's not a usual name, is it? You'd think there must have been relations, friends, somebody, but there wasn't. Poor Litzi. Father managed to make contact with some other dancers, but it was no use. Things must return to normal, one sort of hopes, but in this day and age that's mistaken. We somehow expected her to reappear from the dead, and then instead the Frau Baronin telegraphed.'

In the square in front of the hotel, a statue was flood-lit in the same disfiguring phosphorescent glare, of a Russian soldier cut out of a block of stone twice the size of life, raising a flag high above his head.

The sound of Stavrakis starting the engine to drive Margit home shatters the silence. According to Margit, Russian soldiers are actually garrisoned in the town, but they remain invisible to the population except on Saturday evenings when they descend upon the railway station to drink themselves into a stupor. Whereupon they are chucked like logs into military vans and delivered back to barracks.

'Is there nothing we can do for you ?'

Margit replies, 'The new Larousse would be helpful for my work, but they'd never let me keep the only private copy in western Hungary.'

·Forty Two·

We are in Switzerland. For some time Henriette has been dropping hints about imminent good news. The prospect enlivens her. 'You'll see soon enough,' she says, 'it's in your interest.' She pats my cheeks. *Meshugge*, she calls me, and laughs as though herself startled to retrieve a word in Yiddish out of some sunken recess of the memory.

Oscar and Helga Webber are with us; Oscar in check trousers and summer wind-cheater, with a light blue cap, so that passers-by look him over. Stavrakis is supposed to arrive in town. The entourage is gathering.

'The old lady is truly magnificent,' Oscar says. 'Why, it's wonderful. They don't make them like that any more.'

In front of our hotel is the shore of the lake, with mountains in the distant view. In silver light, gulls wheel and scream. Sailing boats dip at their moorings under the swell of a passenger ferry. An ornamental jet of water soars into the air, and spray from it falls away in a freshening sparkle.

In her room, Henriette is rested and relaxed, in a rightful world of comfort. Her high spirits are infectious. Visitors come to her room for sessions which I may not attend.

'And what is this good news ?'

'Hm, hm, all in its own good time.'

To the best of my recollection, Henriette has never before been to a concert. Now she also visits the city museum, and heads out for the shops in pre-war style, buying this and that with a wave of the hand, Baron Gustav's daughter in a customary dark blue suit and hat to match. We go on expeditions as far afield as the Vierwaldstättersee.

In the years I have known Henriette, she has scarcely aged, to judge by appearances. The curls of her hair are no whiter, the walk is as lively as ever. When she is standing still, she seems poised and vital, not to be budged, her shoulders as square as though she were twenty years younger. Nobody likes to cross her even in trivial matters, which is as well, for loss of temper alone makes her look a woman in her seventies, as in fact is the case. That dreadful sudden blackening around the eyes, the nose as sharp as a bone: rage has the effect of stiffening a death-mask out of her face.

She mourns for Jules, I know, in her fashion. As his own victim, as a tragic individual, a man who made a series of mistakes, who had no need to put himself in the way of that destiny. Blame in her eyes is beside the point. She does not visualise the prisoner in that column, nor hear the train wheels, she cannot put herself in the position of those who had no Perry's Ridge to fall back on, who were doomed to be deported and murdered.

A sentimentalist, she calls me, a worshipper of false gods. Like everybody else ever born, she tells me, you'd have been disappointed in your parents, it's the law of the human species. Personal inadequacy, practically speaking neurosis or even obsession, drives this romanticising of Jules and Litzi. I am not blind to the proportion of truth in what she says.

'Gustav Ellingen was a legend in his day. How was it done?' I have read that portion of the family story to her, and she approves, sentimentalist that she is. And how is it possible to confront her with everything else I have found out or deciphered, to ask for explanations about Rudi and Rex and her own ambivalent sexual behaviour, to bring her to separate the voluntary from the involuntary factors in Jules's death?

I have been confused by her, I will admit, I have certainly been frightened.

'Today's the day,' she says. She hums to herself happily and tunelessly.

Pale haze over the picture postcard lake, the mountain-tops a massive outline, the promise of sun at noon.

In a chauffeur-driven car, we cross the city. Behind spiked iron railings, the bank is more like a private house. The receptionist is in striped trousers and a black tail-coat. The conference room has elaborate furniture, and creamy landscapes to appeal to collectors with a taste for the nineteenth century, but nothing to indicate financial or banking activities. Stavrakis and the Webbers, and a pair of lawyers, a director of the bank, and Henriette chairing a committee meeting, as once at Concordia.

What had happened, in short, was that attitudes towards accounts unclaimed since the war had shifted. Such accounts could now be released to next of kin on condition that the authorities were satisfied that the original owner had been Jewish, and had been murdered in a German camp. 'Beyond reasonable doubt and in accordance with the known facts,' in the words of the lawyers. One such account, opened well before the war and untouched ever since, had belonged to Jules. Out of a folder is lifted correspondence from Margulies, dating back a quarter of a century and more. Here is money from Concordia ; money from Rudi's estate.

Henriette is not going to miss a single nuance expressed on the faces at the table. She leans forward.

'We've been working on this for years.'

'The credit is all yours,' Stavrakis says.

Too moved to speak, Oscar rises and walks round the table, to embrace me.

Forms are produced, a pen is pushed into my hand.

The record shows that Jules never touched this part of his fortune. In practice, the means of saving himself would have lain in these resources. The face of Paul Solkovsky comes to mind. But the pen is open, a finger is pointing at the line, and the banker is saying, 'You have your grandmother to thank, her battle has been sustained and admirable, I am glad that our authorities have at last displayed common sense, we need not go so far as to speak about humanity.'

'You have the Ellingen genes,' Oscar is telling me, 'and now the means as well, there'll be no stopping you.'

'What are you going to do with it ?' Henriette asks. 'What are your plans altogether ?'

Decisions form sometimes before we are consciously aware of them. To live as the child of Jules and Litzi, for their flesh and spirit to survive in the world as it has become.

The flight home finds Henriette still in the best of spirits. Oscar and Helga are with us, Marietta Revertella is to stay the following week. At the onset of summer, Perry's Ridge is beautiful, secluded in greening woods. Newly clipped, the lawn is in perfect condition, in a pattern of stripes left by the mower. Blossom is pink and fluffy on the fruit trees planted by Rex. Correspondence has piled up during Henriette's absence in Switzerland, and she scoops it together. Freda Butley, welcoming, prepares a meal. There is the silver-handled walking stick which has come to me from Rex. What the house misses more than anything is the lurching presence of Robbie the labrador, put to sleep a year ago.

'I want to join our people.'

'Join our people?' Henriette's query is sharp. 'What can you mean?'

Share the experience of the masses. To live as a Jew. *Our people*? In Palestine? Surely not. Nobody goes there. You can't go back on everything that has happened. Repeating my words as though in disbelief, she hardens her mouth, and the lips become thin and livid.

'This is where we are now.'

The sweep of Henriette's hand encompasses the drawing-room, including the portrait of Kismet and the Noble Savage candlesticks, fruit-trees, lawn, countryside, England.

Anger is spurting into her face, draining it, rounding and blackening the eyes; the death-mask forms.

In the garden I catch the scent of wall-flowers. I walk across to the cottage, to find Mrs Whalton submerged in her chair. Susie has a job making cardboard boxes, she has a young man and looks like settling down. To take the path to the village used to feel like an adventure. More rows of houses are visible through the rows of trees than I seem to have remembered, blotching the blues and greens of the lengthening evening shadows. That path will always belong to Rex. Down here he had slipped away for his drinking, hoping in vain that nobody would notice afterwards how he could only poke the food about on his plate, and with what difficulty he was able to climb upstairs. Sure enough, Mr Whalton, his old companion, is at the bar. Only there had been no need to keep up pretences in front of the gardener.

Like Rex in his day, I return a little late. Oscar and Helga are thoroughly frightened. 'Oh Madam is bad,' says Freda Butley, who has stayed on to do the supper, 'I never saw her so poorly, not even when Mr Rex passed away.

We speak in whispers. 'Go and make your peace,' they urge me. 'Apologise. It makes no difference to you, let her have her way.'

As usual when crossed, Henriette has taken to bed. Curtains drawn. The air in the room is impregnated with what must have been a heavy overdose of essence in her bath. The sheets have been laundered and starched to a shine. An arc of light from the bedside table lamp pierces the gloom.

With a limp wrist she gestures me out, and murmurs, 'I'm too tired, much too tired for this.'

Migraine, insomnia, nausea: she complains of the symptoms during such crises, but somehow seems energetic enough in the morning.

Freda Butley has come early to take up a breakfast tray. She says doubtfully, 'Madam is a little stronger today, she's asking for more toast.'

Oscar and Helga are pretending to be interested in the albums in the drawing-room. They talk about misunderstandings, the generation gap, mutual tolerance.

At eleven o'clock I am summoned upstairs. Henriette is leaning back against her pillows. A crocheted shawl. She looks haggard.

People like us, it appeared from what she began to say, are defined only by what we do, not by what we are. I had been brought up here, had even attended the parish church on a Sunday. What kind of identity as a Jew remained? A hundred years ago Gustav Ellingen had been rescued out of the ditch, and who could guess the religion of his unknown parents? *Jude muss man sein aber nicht zum Abattoir*, meaning that the whole thing shouldn't be taken too seriously. A matter of social duty, that's all. It had been expected of her and Rudi, in their position, yes, but they hadn't brought up Jules to be any sort of a Jew. His education had been completely secular, mine even more so. Gustav had been able to recite *Shma Israel Adonai Eloheynu Adonai Echad*, she knew the words, but Jules hadn't, and whatever could I make of it? Could I pray, did I know the first thing about the obligations of the religion, or its even more binding prohibitions? I'd be embarrassed at the sight and sound of it all. *Our people*, indeed. Sharing the experience of the masses! What would happen if I went to Palestine, all right Israel, was that some day soon a war would break out, a gun would be shoved at me, and I would be obliged to shoot some harmless Arab who asked nothing more than to be left in peace. Killer-eyes at large.

'With my back to the afternoon sun.'

'No sooner do I give you a fortune than you round on me, to tear me to pieces. It's not even been a week. This is gratitude for all I've done for you since you landed on my doorstep.'

Killer-eyes, it seems, had been a short-hand but kindly-meant expression for the streak of fanaticism Rex had detected in me. Or lack of balance, to put it more kindly. Look at the way I identified with Jules. We had to come to quite other terms with his death. The wrong was in its nature beyond avenging. Look also at the ridiculous way I had tried to revenge myself on Paul Solkovsky. Who were we to take this wrong upon ourselves? It wasn't decent, it wasn't healthy. In any case, the Jews themselves couldn't want someone who came to them out of the blue, with such motives. I must have picked up cheap notions from the likes of Oscar and Helga, ghetto-types for all their warm hearts. Wasn't it really that girl, the violinist? Stavrakis had warned that I'd run after her. My place was here. How could I contemplate leaving her to play cards with the Englehearts and ginger-haired Dora Esterbrook for the rest of her days?

Truth serves no purpose, of course, it is kinder to pity others and to lie.

'Everything about Perry's Ridge is a falsehood,' I replied, 'or if that's exaggerated, it's artificial.' Altogether an alibi, quite transparent. No use thinking that because she was called Smail-Turner other people were deceived. The Germans hadn't stopped to inquire whether Jules was properly orthodox and obeyed all the religious commandments. Murder would have been her fate too, and mine. It was also obvious why Jules had refused to come to Perry's Ridge. Not willing for a drunken homosexual to be openly living off his mother. Killer-eyes was a phrase designed to test me out, she'd seen for herself how he had tried to molest me that day on the ice. What on earth had made her accept the succession of subterfuges and frauds ? Neither the public school nor the regiment he claimed as his were able to recognise him. Probably Smail-Turner was an invented name.

I stood up to fetch from my room the carefully preserved documents from Oundle and the Durham Light Infantry. Helga and Oscar and Freda Butley had been listening on the far side of the door, they brought the scene to a close. Much too late, I caught sight of the white and decomposed face in the shadows against the pillows, the hooded swollen eyes.

We telephoned Dr Clarke.

'A bit of a rumpus,' the doctor said. 'Quite like old times. Not to worry, I'll pop along with a sedative. Tough as an ox, and actually a good burst of rage does absolute wonders for the heart, it's a tonic.'

Alcohol is available at Perry's Ridge now, and Dr Clarke had a whisky and stayed to lunch. 'All quiet on the domestic front,' he said, 'I'll keep an eye on her.'

In the evening Henriette came downstairs, transformed. She was in dressing-gown and slippers, her smile was radiant. In her hand was a letter, and she held it out to us without comment.

The Stuttgart City Museum had been writing to her. While carrying out a routine examination of that part of the collection which was not on display, a picture had been discovered in the stacks. This picture, by J.J.Lecomte-du-Nouy, was described under the title 'A Prince of the Desert'. There was no record of how the picture had reached the museum, its provenance was uncertain, but it appeared to be one among several pictures looted from Vienna in the Second World War. A label had been discovered on the stretcher, to the effect that the picture had been sold in Paris in 1892, becoming the property of Baron Gustav Ellingen of Schloss Pernsdorf, in Vienna. Addressing himself to Pernsdorf, the museum curator had been happy to learn the name and present address of Baron Ellingen's daughter and heir. Upon confirmation of ownership, the museum would undertake the steps necessary for restitution.

All these years later, Baron Gustav is looking after his own – Henriette is convinced of it. In the sequence of events leading to the recovery of this picture there has to be a will, an intention. The famous Arab prince is animate, like someone in the family coming home after a long absence. If need be, the ceiling will have to be taken down to fit the picture in, or an addition built on to Perry's Ridge.

The anger has passed.

'Go on, go on, go on,' she says to me. 'Go away wherever you want.'

Marietta is coming, the two will live as sisters. Henriette says, 'I'll play cards with Dora Esterbrook every day if I must. I'm taken care of, I'm fine. Away with you.'

Nothing lasts like courage. Nothing lasts except courage.

About the Author

David Pryce-Jones was born in Vienna in 1936, and educated at Eton and Oxford. The author of some fourteen books, he has worked as a journalist and taught in various universities in the United States. He lives in London with his wife and three children.